A spiritually enlightening self-help book

A Novel

A WALK *with* JOHN

THE POWER OF LOVE AND HATE

Dr. Lauren Ball

Because of the dynamic nature of the Internet, any web addresses or links contained in this book may have changed since publication and may no longer be valid. The views expressed in this work are solely those of the author and do not necessarily reflect the views of the publisher, and the publisher hereby disclaims any responsibility for them.

ISBN: 979-8-88945-113-6 (paperback)
ISBN: 979-8-88945-115-0 (hardback)
eISBN: 979-8-88945-114-3

Brilliant Books Literary
137 Forest Park Lane Thomasville
North Carolina 27360 USA

Printed in the United States of America

I t is essential that we understand why we are placed here on earth so that we may conduct our lives in a manner conducive to re-qualifying for residence with God.

We cannot hide behind our ignorance when the information for our spiritual growth is available. If we ignore these criteria, we should not expect to receive the same blessings and spiritual advancement as do those who embrace the teachings laid out in the scriptures.

This book was written to aid readers in their sincere search for enlightenment. The insights herein will help them integrate their lives more harmoniously with others and draw them closer to God.

The true meanings of "love" and "hate" are explained here in a surprising, comprehensive, and edifying manner, leaving no doubt as to what is required for the readers' ultimate residence with their creator.

Satan's true, evil purposes also are revealed, along with the weapons he uses in his attempts to bring about human destruction. God's weapons to combat the terrible influences Satan brings to bear also are extensively discussed.

An in-depth discussion of many other ideas also is presented for a greater understanding of why we are really here on earth.

I believe this book was written with inspiration and guidance from above. The character of John represents the inspiration and guidance I have received as I have pondered the complex subjects presented in this work. Although John doesn't really exist, he portrays the inspiration we all are promised if we obey the commandments that help us get through this life. I believe the concepts presented here are viable and true. Of course, we all have our agency, the God-given right to make our own choices, and it is our right to choose not to accept these concepts. I do hope that these words will have a positive impact on those who are truly searching for truth and spiritual enlightenment and who, through their own efforts, can make this world a better place.

The contents of this book come from the experiences, opinions, and precepts garnered from a lifetime of prayer, dreams, meditation, inspiration, personal revelation, and study.

The major thrust of this book is to encourage everyone to live the laws of love. According to Christ, these are the greatest commandments given to humankind, and on them hang all the other laws and commandments He has given us. (Mark 12:30-31) There isn't much time left for the human race in this phase of our existence. Christ will soon return and call us to account for the condition of the earth and for our own lives. It is my prayer that all of us will examine our relationships with God, others, and the earth itself, and create a unity, a oneness, with all.

All scriptural references in this book are taken from the King James Version of the Bible.

Dedication

I dedicate this book to all seekers who, dissatisfied with the explanations of this life given by their ecclesiastical leaders, have the courage and desire to seek out for themselves the truths found in the literary and religious works of this world.

Acknowledgments

I wish to thank my lovely wife, Geri, for the many hours she spent editing this work. I also wish to thank my brothers, Elwyn, Leslie, and Rulon, and my sister, Loree, for their encouragement, suggestions, and support throughout the writing and editing of this book.

Disclaimer

The contents and concepts in this book are not specific to any particular religion, sect, or group.

Any resemblance in this book to real persons, living or dead, is purely coincidental.

Introduction

When Moses came down from the mountain with the stone plates containing the Ten Commandments, he had a glow about him, a brightness that frightened the Israelites (Exod. 34:29–34).

Every day we see people who seem to have a natural brightness, a light that surrounds them and sets them apart from others. It is a light that seems to come from within, and that radiates outward to form an atmosphere about such people. There is a kind, peaceful, understanding quality these people possess that attracts others to them. It is this feeling that needs to be brightened and magnified in each of us until, as with our Savior and God the Father, it becomes brighter than the noonday sun.

Conversely, there are those who seem to be encircled about by a darkness that drives others away. These are people who have shunned the powers of light and righteousness. They go the way of the world and seek to gratify themselves; they lust after the pleasures of the moment. There is no place in their lives for our Lord and Savior. Their agency, or freedom of choice, has been used to choose the path of least resistance—the path of darkness, self-gratification, and destruction.

We each create and project our own aura by the choices we make. In some of us, it is bright, lighting up the lives of those with whom we associate. In others, it is a small, dark emanation that casts long shadows of disharmony, contention, violence, and confusion. It is the intent of this book to help each of us intensify and increase the projection of our own light in a righteous and positive manner. This illumination will then increase in brightness and intensity as we become more perfected, embracing the concepts of love, charity, humility, and righteousness, and expunging destructive traits such as anger, greed, procrastination, and so on.

If we can increase the brightness of our spheres of influence each day of our lives by magnifying our stewardships here on earth, we will be doing as our Father in heaven has commanded. Our radiance can become as bright as His and can reach outward to all those who seek righteousness and perfection.

At some point in our existence, many of us ponder the meaning of life, and look inward for the answers to some of its most perplexing questions:

1. Who am I?
2. What am I?
3. Where am I?
4. Why am I?
5. Where did I come from?
6. Why am I here?
7. Where am I going?
8. What must I do to get there?

When seriously considered, these are questions that lead to a quest for the truth. When answered with truth, and when we apply that truth correctly, these questions can change our lives, allowing us to set and attain productive goals that make of us eternal winners in this game of life. These questions also help us base our goals on those spiritual values that will allow us to reside with our Father in Heaven once again.

Each of these questions will be answered here, but most only with simplified answers. To expand our comprehension, we must search and study the scriptures diligently. Fasting and prayerful meditation also are essential to the understanding of God's works. If we really want our studies to have a great spiritual impact on our lives, we must make a *serious commitment* to obey God's laws and commandments. We must truly follow Him as He has directed.

For some of the questions, an expanded answer will be given in these pages. A careful study of this book should inspire a desire to set aside a portion of each day to meditate and ponder the knowledge God has given through the scriptures and other good books to help us master our lives while here on earth.

Opening our minds to truth is essential as we strive for wisdom and righteousness. Whenever we study, whether this or another book, we should always pray to God for an understanding of the truths contained therein. We must then listen to the promptings of the Holy Spirit for confirmation or denial. Truth is manifested only through this avenue. When we assume that the answers, we receive come from Him, without first praying to God, we may very well be misled by the powers of darkness. God cannot lie; Satan is always misleading. So, when we try to understand the things of God without true humility, without an open mind, or without prayer, we will surely be misled.

God loves us all equally. He does not, however, love all our actions equally. Therein lies the only difference between the murderer and the saint. It is this distinction that ultimately will determine the degrees of glory we will inherit. For we each will be judged by our works; by the degree of our repentance, and by what we have become compared to what we would have become had we followed the admonitions of our Savior.

This work is designed to help set the goals necessary to gain the highest degree in the Celestial Kingdom. To aim for anything less would be to deny God, Christ, and the Holy Spirit, and the glorious purpose for which they sent us here. It also would mean that we were too lazy and slothful to care whether or not we even entered one of the kingdoms, or that we were not interested in setting the goals that would expedite our progress and spiritual growth. I pray that we will accept nothing less than the best efforts of which we are capable. My search to find these universal guidelines has taken me through the scriptures many times, through many good and revealing books, and especially through much meditation and prayer. The answers have come slowly, one at a time, over a period of many years. Sometimes the answers have come because of traumatic experiences in my life. Usually they have come because of my persistence in pursuing and seeking out answers, but I feel they have always come through inspiration from God. To some, these guideposts may seem overly simplistic and of little value. Continued study and application, however, will reveal the tremendous impact these answers can have on our lives when acted upon correctly. While some readers may not believe in God, they still should not deny the value of following the precepts upon which this work is based. In so doing, their quality of life can be considerably improved, human suffering can be diminished, and happiness and contentment can be increased far beyond imagining. Embracing these concepts will help balance life and put goals in the proper perspective, thus giving a worthy purpose to life.

We must seriously ponder in our hearts the answers to these questions:

1. **Who am I?** I am a child of God. I am a distinct personality, separate from all others. I am the sum total of all the knowledge, experience, beliefs, and belief systems I have embraced as well as the thinking of my past. I am loved by God. Before I came to earth, I was a spirit child of God.

2. **What am I?** I am what I have made of myself. By the choices I have made, using my thoughts and actions, I have become a physically, mentally, and spiritually unique personality. I am responsible for the "me" I have created and will continue to create because God has given me one of the greatest of all gifts: the right to choose for myself what I want to be—good, evil, productive, nonproductive, or counterproductive. This freedom to choose is known as "agency." Though I have allowed others to influence some

of my actions and my thinking, still I am the one responsible for what I have become. I cannot foist the blame on others—not my parents, not my peers, not my brothers and sisters, and not others who have played a part in my upbringing. When I reached maturity, I not only assumed responsibility for my future actions, but I also relinquished the right to blame anyone else for what I have become.

3. **Where am I?** I am on the planet earth and, in the continuum of time, somewhere between the preexistent spirit world and the paradise of the millennium. I am somewhere between total evil and total righteousness or, perfection. I am in a state somewhere between forgiveness and unforgiveness, between complete repentance and total un-repentance. I hope to be in a state of complete repentance before I die. I realize that I will be judged by what I have become and not by whether the good I have accomplished outweighs the sins I have committed.

4. **Why am I?** I am because God created me and loves me. I am so that by exercising my agency, in a righteous manner, I may again live with my heavenly Father. I am so that I may, through righteous endeavors, become a perfected being as God has commanded (Matt. 5:48). I am so that I might have joy.

5. **Where did I come from?** Before I was born into this world, I was a spirit child of God. I resided in the pre-mortal existence, where I was taught those things necessary to prepare me for this life. How well I learned and embraced God's laws and commandments, and the degree of my commitment and obedience, helped to determine the status and circumstances into which I was born. Those factors also helped determine what opportunities I would be afforded in this life.

6. **Why am I here?** I am here to work out my salvation and exaltation. I am here to overcome temptation, to learn obedience, to gain all of the knowledge and experience I can while in this world, and to seek out the truth wher-

ever I can find it. I am here to overcome adversity, subdue the earth and all of my destructive traits, and learn total self-discipline. I am here to perfect my body, mind, and spirit to the greatest extent possible. I also am here to become a productive member of society and to give of my talents for the general welfare of humankind. I am here to help others in every way I can, especially to aid them in working out their salvation and in drawing close to God in every way.

7. **Where am I going when I leave here?** Where I go depends largely on what I do while I am here. "In my Father's house are many mansions: if it were not so, I would have told you. I go to prepare a place for you." (John 14:2) Where I go depends on how I treat my fellow man, the degree of my perfection, the extent of my repentance, the degree I embrace all of Gods laws and commandments and accept His ordinances. With an absolute and sure knowledge of Christ, I could be cast into outer darkness if I then choose to worship Satan completely. Or I could inherit one of the kingdoms of God: The Telestial the lowest Kingdom, the Terrestrial or middle Kingdom, or even the Celestial or highest Kingdom. The Bible is replete with scriptures on the judgment. I will be judged according to my works, good or evil. The Kingdom I inherit will depend on my thoughts and actions while here on earth. I alone am responsible because I have exercised my freedom to choose as I have seen fit therefore, I must be prepared to accept what the judgment dictates. I must never forget that in spite of all I can do and I must never quit striving it is the redemption of Jesus Christ that makes it possible for me to work out my salvation.

8. **What must I do to get there?** I must strive with all my strength, heart and soul to be obedient, to put the things of God first in my life. I must be in a constant state of repentance, embrace the principles of love and follow all the concepts God has given us in the scriptures. I must

never forget that as a child of God I owe my first and last loyalty to Him. I must serve mankind and learn to love as God has loved. I must make hope, humility, meekness, and charity a very real part of my life. I cannot procrastinate the day of my repentance and expect to receive the fullness of God's blessings or expect to have the same degree of perfection as those who live in a state of Grace.

This book is a selection of basic and essential guideposts to give an understanding of why we are here and what spiritual paths are necessary to gain the greatest possible growth and perfection; road markers with which we can identify regardless of who we are, what our backgrounds are, or from where we came.

Certain assumptions are necessary to help understand this work. First: God placed humans here for a specific purpose. Second: This purpose must be consistent with the teachings of the holy scriptures. Third: This purpose must be attainable, easily understood, and compatible with the commandments God has given us. When we accept and continue to strive to fulfill the purpose for which He sent us, we will reap all the eternal blessings He has promised to those who are obedient and faithful.

The following terms are defined to help readers understand this material and appreciate the meaning intended by the author. These terms may have a slightly different meaning when applied to matters outside this work.

Agency: The God-given right to respond to good or evil, and the willingness to accept responsibility for God's rewards or punishments earned thereby. In other words, the right to choose, to make decisions as we see fit for any given set of circumstances, whether they be good or evil or some shade in between. There are people who seem unwilling to accept responsibility for their agency; nevertheless, when they appear before the bar on judgment day, they will be held accountable for the development and use of their agency. They will not be allowed to place blame on others whose decisions they accepted and embraced.

Perfection: That which is without blemish, has all knowledge, all truth, all power, all faith, all control, is absolutely just and merciful, and exemplifies all goodness, patience, and long-suffering. A person possessing the quality of perfection will have subdued every nonproductive and counterproductive characteristic, trait, and need, and will have complete control and discipline over these. He will have perfected every one of the productive characteristics, traits, and needs, and will have all the qualities, power, and glory that are exemplified in Jesus Christ.

Productivity: Those thoughts and actions that lead to righteous accomplishments and growth toward perfection.

Nonproductivity: Those thoughts and actions that are passive with regard to our growth toward perfection, and that allow us to slide toward destruction.

Counterproductivity: Those thoughts and actions that lead to unrighteous acts and accomplishments, and that are destructive to growth toward perfection.

The purpose of life: To embrace and act upon everything that will perfect our bodies, minds, and spirits, and to follow the plan of salvation that God has outlined in the scriptures. Also, to strive for entrance into the highest kingdom of glory, the Celestial Kingdom (Matt. 5:48).

Personality: The unique individuality embodied in each person. It is affected and molded by our experiences, thoughts, characteristics, and traits, and by our mental, physical, and spiritual needs.

Characteristics: Those elements that make up our personalities: appetites, attitudes, attributes, emotions, habits, and talents.

Traits: Those elements that make up our characteristics: love, hate, humility, greed, kindness, and so on.

Basic needs: Those physical, mental, and spiritual needs that we all have. When developed properly, these needs balance our personalities and help us become the most productive individuals within the range of our capabilities.

Intelligence: The ever-increasing ability to use, in wisdom and righteousness, our knowledge, experience, and agency. This helps us to mature and be perfected in all phases and states of our existence.

It also increases the control we have over our environment in a productive way.

Determining the truth: There is a method of determining the truth of all things, whether from God, humans, or Satan. This applies to books, scriptures, talks, political candidates, or anything about which there is a question.

When we approach God in prayer, desiring to know the truth, we often do so in such a haphazard way that we are unable to discern the answer when it comes. We all have our prejudices, or certain issues about which our minds are closed; when we kneel to pray, these factors interfere with and cloud our minds. For instance, if I were the one responsible for hiring and firing personnel within an organization, and I was prejudiced against a certain race, there would be few of that race working for me. Even if an applicant against whom I was prejudiced was the better-qualified of two applicants, and I prayed about which one I should hire, my prejudice would cloud the answer I received.

The desire to know the truth, or mind of God, requires that we completely open our minds to all possibilities when we pray. If we entertain any doubts or possess any predetermined attitudes concerning the subject of prayer, we will surely be misled by the powers of darkness. For graver issues, we also should include a 24-hour fast and a period of meditating preparation prior to prayer. Also essential is the suspension or elimination of all prejudice and negative feelings pertaining to the subject matter. We must open our minds for the truth. This applies to anything we read.

Suppose I desire to know whether or not the Bible is the word of God. If I possess a predetermined opinion that it is untrue, being so told by my parents, I may well be misled by my negative attitude and will probably never know the truth. If I pray believing that an opinion is true or false I may still be misled.

On the other hand, if I precede my prayer with fasting and meditation, open my mind to all possibilities, and relinquish my prejudice, the Holy Spirit can then manifest the truth to me. I will feel a burning in my bosom, a feeling that the Bible is God's word. If it is not true, I will have a very negative feeling.

It is always necessary to read, study, and pray when we are seeking the truth about something. Those steps ensure that the Holy Spirit will manifest the truth to us. If fasting and prayer are done with a sincere desire to know, with an open mind, and without positive or negative prejudice, an answer will come. If the fasting and prayer are accompanied by a closed mind, predetermined negative attitudes, or any kind of prejudice, the powers of darkness will take over.

It is not easy to remove prejudice and open our minds to the influence of the Holy Ghost. It is equally difficult to change attitudes or mindsets that prevent our understanding and acceptance of the truth. But if we do not make these changes, our souls may be lost. Learning to rely on God's inspiration and strength will help us overcome these terrible influences, and we can then differentiate between the influences of good and evil in our minds.

Sometimes we try with our limited and ineffectual minds to define God's plans for humankind. We may say that this book or that book is or isn't true. But can we, in wisdom, state that God has given the world no revelation other than that found in the Bible, and that He will give no more in the future? "And other sheep I have, which are not of this fold: them also I must bring, and *they shall hear my voice*; and there shall be one fold, and one shepherd" (John 10:16). Moreover, thou son of man, take thee one stick, and write upon it, For Judah, and for the children of Israel his companions: then take another stick, and write upon it, For Joseph, the stick of Ephraim, and for all the house of Israel his companions: (Ezekiel 37:16) This indicates that God has given His word to others.

How do we know what God has done in the past or what He will do in the centuries to come? Are we in possession of all of the knowledge about Him and His plans for us? Are we really foolish enough to believe that we know all there is to know about God, or that He has revealed all He is going to reveal? This is God's world, not ours. God does what He wants to do, and when we presuppose that He has done all He is going to do, we err greatly.

I cannot and will not place limitations on what I believe God has done or not done. I have studied and prayed, and I accept as truth the revelations He has given us. There does appear to be a period of about 2,000 years in which we had no revelations. This doesn't mean that there weren't any, or that there won't be any in the future. God can do what He pleases when He pleases. I am not about to second-guess Him and put my salvation on the line. When our minds are open to truth, we can receive either confirmation or denial of the issue at stake—especially if we are sincere in our desire to know, and we follow the law of fasting and prayer.

It may be difficult for many of us to understand or accept the possibility that we can be deceived by Satan and the powers of darkness. But, make no mistake: Satan influences us in every way he can. He not only will put temptation into our minds, but he also will inspire us with destructive and false revelation. His repertoire for deceiving humankind is virtually unlimited. His influence on our minds is just as real and just as powerful as is the influence of the forces of good. It has to be this way, for otherwise our freedom of choice would be impaired. That is why the method for receiving inspiration from God has very strict guidelines. When we don't follow it explicitly, we open the door for Satan to influence the answers to our prayers. If we follow these guidelines, we can know the truth or falseness of all things.

In summary, these are the steps necessary to receive inspiration from God and determine the truth of all things:

1. Create a desire to know the truth concerning God's works.
2. For issues that may affect our salvation, fast and meditate for at least twenty-four hours prior to prayer.
3. Begin and end the fast with sincere prayer.
4. Develop an open mind and cast aside all positive or negative prejudices and predetermined attitudes.
5. Pray with a humble and contrite heart, and with a sincere desire to know the truth about that for which you are praying and to have that truth manifested. Include in your prayer that you will feel a burning in your bosom if truth exists, and that a confusion of thought will be present if it does not exist.

6. Wait quietly and meditatively for the answer to come. It may come quickly, but often it takes a while. Do not be impatient. Just keep studying and meditating, and the answer will come. God loves us all and He will not let us down. Sometimes a trial of our faith will precede the answer, but if we are persistent, it will come.

The character of John in this book represents the inspiration, guidance, and revelation that I believe was present in producing this book. Therefore, John was created as a teaching mechanism to convey the lessons necessary to help increase our spirituality and bring us closer to both God and one another.

John

He was just sitting on a rock, as if deep in thought.

I had driven up from Buena Vista, Colorado, and was preparing to hike in the mountains near Ptarmigan Lake. There were no other vehicles around, so I assumed this man had walked up here from somewhere down below. I put on my backpack and started up the trail leading to the pass overlooking the Ptarmigan Lake valley. Savoring the brisk air and awesome scenery, I was looking forward to enjoying some quiet time and meditation while I walked.

As I started to walk by this gentleman, he looked up and gave me a disarming smile.

"Hi," he said.

"Hi, yourself," I returned. "You must have gotten up early to beat me here."

"I guess you could say that" he said. "I've been waiting for you for some time now."

"Huh?" I said, feeling a little foolish. "You've been waiting for me? I don't even know you."

"Nevertheless, I've been asked to meet you here," he said.

"There must be some mistake," I said. "I wasn't planning to meet anyone. I just came up here to enjoy the beautiful scenery and do some meditating."

"Your name is Lauren, isn't it?" he said, more as a statement than a question.

"Y-yes," I stammered. "Should I know you? Who are you, anyway?"

"Just call me John," he replied.

I was ready to brush off the incident as a prank set up by a friend, but when I started up the trail, John arose and followed me.

He proved to be more agile than I, and as we walked and conversed that day, he showed no sign of fatigue. This was, indeed, an exceptional man. As we talked, his intelligence, wisdom, and understanding of life proved far superior to that of anyone I have ever known. I never did find out from where he came.

As he arose, I got a better look at him. His eyes immediately caught my attention. They were deep azure, with a scintillating quality that seemed to pierce the very depths of my soul, almost as if he could read my mind. He seemed to radiate confidence and power—yet also kindness, compassion, gentleness, wisdom, and knowledge. His features were soft and amiable, and his beautiful white hair and flowing white beard gave him a distinguished air. His timeless visage and demeanor indicated no specific age. "Where are you going?" he asked.

"Just up the trail to hike and enjoy the mountains," I replied.

"They are beautiful, aren't they?" he said. "This is one of my favorite areas, and in the spring it's always spectacular. Do you mind if I join you?"

"That would be g-great," I stammered. I was somewhat taken aback, yet somehow, I found myself looking forward to his company. "Now perhaps you will tell me what this is all about."

"What's what all about?" he asked with a twinkle in his eye.

"You said you were asked to meet me here. Who sent you? Why were you supposed to meet me?" I returned, a little miffed.

"First," he said, "why did you come up here this morning?"

"Well, I just wanted to think about my life," I said.

"That's interesting. What do you think this life is all about?" he asked, with another disarming smile.

"What's that got to do with why you were supposed to meet me here today?" I asked.

"All right," he said, still smiling. "I can't tell you who sent me, but I was sent here to meet you and answer any questions you might have, about life or anything else."

"Are you sure you weren't sent by my friends as a joke?" Yet I knew immediately that he hadn't been.

"No," he smiled, "they didn't send me."

I wasn't sure whether or not to believe him, but I decided to take the chance that he was telling the truth, so I dove in.

"Well, then," I said as we sauntered along the trail leading up to the pass, "how can I make my life more meaningful? And what should I do with the rest of it? I would like to know what my mental and spiritual capacities and capabilities are, and where I will go after I die, and whether or not I would be in the presence of God, and what it means to be one with Him." It all suddenly came out in a rush.

"Hold on just a minute," he said. "Those are noble questions, but are you sure you don't already know the answers?"

"I'm sure I don't," I answered. "This life is more than confusing, and I sense that there's some specific way, or path, we need to take to get back to God, but I'm just not sure how to find it."

"Without knowing the exact pathway to take, the best you can do is wander around a lot or stay in the same place spiritually," he laughed. "Your spiritual growth and the level of perfection you attain in this life determine the opportunities you will be afforded in the next stage of existence. In fact, your whole life is nothing more than a preparation for what comes after death. It requires some very specific decisions and actions while you're here, and a very different mindset from the world in general. The pathway to God does exist, but it may not be easy to find. Very few have been able to break the barriers of tradition and expand their minds enough to search for the answers. But this universe is full of limitless possibilities and potential for those who reach out, expand, and continue to grow and search."

"Well, I'm not quite ready to cash it in yet," I laughed. "I think I have a few good years left in me."

"How can, you be sure?" he answered soberly.

"No one can be sure of how long this life will last," I said, "I suppose we just have to do the best we can while we're here."

I contemplated what he had said for a while. It had the ring of truth and I wanted to believe him. Who *was* this man, anyway, and what was he doing here in the mountains? Why was *I* here in the mountains at this specific time? Was it just a coincidence?

I'm not much of a believer in coincidence. I had felt a deep need to come up here today, but I hadn't expected to meet anyone.

I tried to gather my thoughts. Perhaps he could answer some of the other questions I had as well.

The Rockies were exceptionally beautiful that morning. The air was clean and crisp; the breeze was gentle, almost as if everything in the world waited in anticipation. We paused for a few moments at the pass, enjoying the scenery, before heading on down to the lake.

"Where do you hail from?" I asked nonchalantly

"Well, I guess you could say the world is my home," John replied. "Part of what I do is answer questions to help enlighten people. Today I will answer some of your questions and, of course, enjoy the mountain scenery. Perhaps I can clear up some of your confusion.

"I must ask a very special favor of you, though. Everything we will discuss is very important for humankind, and so I would ask that you make every effort to publish and disseminate, in every way you can, the information I give you today. It is not just for you. It could have a profound impact on some very special people who are greatly in need of this knowledge. Will you make that promise?" he asked.

I really didn't understand what was going on, but I decided to follow my instincts and see what happened. How would this affect my life? How would I know if what he said was the truth? My head was in a whirl.

I waited a few moments, trying to collect my thoughts, wondering what I should ask, intuitively knowing that I was on the verge of finding long-sought answers to questions that had troubled me.

I decided I should be very explicit in what I asked. I was concerned about what harm might result from placing my trust in John. Who would it hurt? It might be prudent to wait and see what he had to offer.

CHAPTER TWO

Bodies and Spirits

"I'm no writer, but I will do my best to publish what I learn today," I promised.

The first question that came to mind was one that I had reflected on many times, but about which I had come to no definite conclusion.

"I have often wondered why God put us here," I said. "And also, what is the relationship between our bodies and our spirits? Do we, as spiritual entities, really need our bodies?"

"You sure get down to the basics in a hurry," John laughed. "Why you are on earth, or why you exist as a human, can only be comprehended when you have a complete understanding of your spiritual form.

"Human spirits are eternal entities. They have memories and experiences that go back through the eternities. More recently, God and His angels, in preparation for humans' physical existence here, have instructed these spirits with the information they need to reside on earth. Though each spirit is a separate entity, all spirits are integrated into a whole, a network of love and knowledge with a singularity of purpose: to grow toward perfection and become one with

God. While in human form, your spirit should try to learn, accept, and express God's love and desires for you, and to bring this form into alignment with God's purpose and mission for it. But because you have your agency—your freedom to choose—this doesn't always happen. In fact, as often as not, human spirits rebel and take the wrong road, leaving them at odds with God's purpose and mission for them.

"The human form is not just a body with a spirit, but rather an eternal spirit that inhabits a very fragile and expendable body—a physical temple of God, as it were—for a very brief period in the eternities. The most important goals of this life are first, to learn to freely accept God's love, to magnify that love, and to unconditionally express it, through service and caring, to all of God's children and to yourself. And secondly, to become obedient to His laws and commandments, which were presented to humans so that they would have a measure of love in action; a feel for the love He has for us. They were also given to expand your understanding and reduce the limits with which you surround yourselves.

"There is always a very delicate balance between the forces of good and evil in your lives," John continued. "These forces are absolutely necessary for humans to have complete freedom to choose their thoughts and actions, and to have the maximum spiritual growth possible. If God allowed the scales to be tipped in favor of either force, life would have no meaning. Humans seldom realize this, so they often make decisions that form beliefs, attitudes, and habits that are contradictory to the forces and energies of life. These beliefs and attitudes then control their intentions, which are the basis for all their actions.

"Besides life, another of God's great gifts is the freedom to choose, which is called 'agency.' The intentions you develop from your use of agency form the basis of your pleasures and miseries in this life. If your pleasures derive from hate, violence, unforgiveness, or any of the evils of the world, and if you remain in this state until death, then these things will rule your existence on the other side. Conversely, if you embrace the things of the spirit, such as love, compassion, and forgiveness, then these will rule your life on the other side. Each time you lie, cheat, steal, hate or hurt someone, and so on, you embed your intentions more deeply within your physical and spiritual brains, until it becomes next to impossible to change your life without professional or godly intervention.

"One of the most important and arduous tasks you have in this life is to bring your body and your spirit into alignment with God's purpose and mission for you. The spirit is the conscience, the consciousness, and the awareness you enjoy in your everyday life. Your experiences are its experiences, your memories, its memories. To gain perfection, your body and spirit must work in harmony with God and the Holy Spirit, both of whom help us understand, know, and discern the truth in all situations. You must, through repentance, become as a little child, innocent through repentance and perfected in Christ. You also must try to overcome and rise above all the distractions and detractors you face in this life.

"Your spirits are not yet perfect, or this life would have no purpose," he continued. "Everyone must undergo the trials and experiences of life to learn obedience and love. You must learn to trust the wisdom behind God's laws and commandments so that obedience will come naturally.

"Some spirits have serious problems overcoming the wants and needs of the physical body. They desire to experience and taste it all, good and bad, regardless of whom they may hurt. The body often rebels against spiritual growth, which appears to be too confining or too hard to attain. Your mind resists making the effort necessary to gain the knowledge that leads to eternal life with God. It wants to live life on its own terms, being submissive and obedient only when it deems it profitable or desires to do so, not heeding the promptings of the Holy Spirit.

"In the preexistence, spirits help to select their earthly parents within parameters dictated by God, and each is assigned to a fetus at conception. Within the boundaries of predetermined spiritual needs, your spirit directs the growth and all functions of the fetal life form, and so becomes a co-creator with God in the creation of your body. All this is done to satisfy a spirit's basic need for the greatest spiritual growth in accordance with all past experiences. Sometimes a spirit agrees to come to earth in a physically or mentally disabled state to maximize the growth of others. The spiritual-growth needs of such a spirit have already been satisfied, and the spirit's inheritance in the highest kingdom of God is assured.

"This human form, from birth to death, is besieged with all of the sensory information, beliefs, and belief systems of family, friends, and society. These beliefs may have originated many generations before, then been handed down by parents, teachers, spiritual leaders, and the world in general, until they become lodged within your physical and spiritual mind, controlling much of your thinking, intentions, and actions. With all these deep-seated traditions, the sensory input, the physical wants and needs that must be satisfied, and all the destructive belief systems, it is no wonder that the spirit has such a difficult time communicating with its human host. Controlling and rising above this physical world is never an easy task, but one that must be done to the greatest degree possible if you are to accomplish your mission and reach your spiritual goal in this life.

"To answer the last part of your question," John said, "the spirit, does, indeed, have need of the body. Eventually the spirit and body will be reunited in a process called 'the resurrection,' and together they will form a unit that is far greater than the sum of their parts. When working together, and in harmony with the laws of love and God's commandments, there is no limit to what a perfected eternal being can accomplish and create."

I pondered this for a few minutes. I could see that I had not been too cooperative with my spirit, and not as obedient to God's commandments as I needed to be to bring my spirit into alignment with its and God's purpose for me. I felt a pang of guilt for all the procrastinating I had done in the past. I resolved to listen more closely to the promptings of the spirit, and to be more obedient.

By this time, we had arrived at the lake.

"I don't believe I've ever seen it so beautiful and peaceful," I commented.

"I don't believe I have, either. Look! There's an eagle over that peak!" John exclaimed, pointing. We watched as the bird circled and flew low over the lake, looking for fish.

"Well," John said after the eagle had disappeared, "is there anything else you were wondering about?"

"I could probably keep you here for a week," I laughed. "You mentioned that God has a purpose and mission for us. Can you tell me what they are?"

"God's full purpose for humankind is not for me to say at this time," John replied. "However, the major purpose is to learn, as Christ taught, to love God with all your might, mind, and soul, and to learn to love others unconditionally, regardless of race, color, nationality, creed, social status, or any other characteristic. All men, women, and children on this earth are brothers and sisters, with an invisible bond or spiritual connection of love. Each person on this earth has the same value in the eyes of God. 'He is no respecter of persons.' (Acts 10:34) No one has the right or the authority to place himself or herself above or below anyone else. God does not love some people more because of their religion, status, race, or color, or for any other reason. He does not hold a king or a president in higher esteem than He does the lowliest peon. He does, however, place a value on humans' actions. He does not condone wars or killing for any reason, especially in the name of religion, unless, in His great wisdom, He needs to accomplish one of His goals.

"Because of the spiritual bond of love among all humankind, what you do to one, you do to all; and what you do to one, you also do to Christ. Your thoughts are transmitted to and magnified in one another, and are felt by everyone in a very real, spiritual sense. You—collectively and individually—become whatever you think about and dwell on the most. Your thought processes can spawn hate, and produce rapists, murderers, adulterers, thieves, and so on. You can sink to the lowest depths of the vilest of beasts or rise to the heights of the gods. Since you can train yourself to completely control your thinking, you also control your destiny, and therefore you are completely accountable for your every act. In other words, you are the creator of your own life by your own thought processes, and by the concepts and beliefs you adopt from others. Your parents are not to blame. Neither are your teachers, spiritual leaders, or peers. All reasoning individuals on earth are responsible for what they are and become by the choices they make. When you completely assume full responsibility for yourself and realize that you are the product of your thinking, judgments, and decisions, you will have the maturity to start creating your life the way you need to to have the same purpose for yourself as your spirit and God. In other words, you will control your own destiny and your own growth.

"You are the total and unequivocal product of your own thought processes, intentions, and judgments that created the belief systems you employ throughout life. It is impossible for someone else to assume this responsibility or to be blamed," John stated.

I considered this for a moment. This meant I could no longer blame my parents or anyone else for who I was. It's true that they had an influence on my life, but the mental processing of their teachings and punishments were all up to me.

Not being able to shift the responsibility to others made me feel a little uncomfortable. Then I realized that I didn't want to assume responsibility for the actions of my children, either, after they had been taught the correct principles by which to live. A new light dawned in me: in actuality, I can neither shift the accountability for my actions onto someone else, nor assume it for others.

CHAPTER THREE

Love

By this time my stomach was growling. I opened my backpack and offered John a sandwich and a bottle of water, which he gratefully accepted.

As we ate, I carefully considered my next question.

"What are love and charity?" I asked, hoping for more enlightenment.

"You really are eager, aren't you?" he laughed. "I can't even finish my sandwich before your next question."

"I'm sorry," I said. "I don't mean to be so pushy, but I am anxious to learn as much as I can. I may never have this chance again."

"I understand," he said with a twinkle in his eye. "But who knows? We may meet again."

He sat quietly for a few minutes as we watched some ducks dive for food on the other side of the lake.

After he finished his sandwich, he said, "There are many kinds of love. There is the love parents have for their children, and they for their parents. There is the passion of first love; the love for animals; the love for friends. Lust is a form of selfish love, the need for sexual gratification. To make it more complicated, love varies in intensity among individuals, depending on how much they have been able to accept from God. However, all types of love have some common denominators that we will discuss later. By its very nature, unshared, unexpressed, and unnurtured love will diminish and die.

"Love and charity are very simple and yet very complex—and not at all what you may have been led to believe. I'll try to explain each of these concepts in turn so you'll have a better understanding of their nature and how they can affect your life.

"Love is the greatest and most powerful force in the universe. It is the essence of life and emanates directly from God, encircling and permeating each of you. To the extent that you accept it, you can express it. Its elements are service-oriented and composed of the great unifying and cohesive forces of the universe, binding all spiritual and physical matter together. Love, with all its elements, is the power by which God has created His whole physical and spiritual universe. Love is the power that brings purpose to all things, for both God and humankind. It is that power you must learn to accept and express toward God, others, and self—in that order.

"By using love in every aspect of your life, you eventually may learn to create and express physical matter from spiritual matter, as do God and Christ. God is love, and the more you learn to love as God loves, the more righteous, powerful, and Godlike you become. As you accept this love from God and Christ, you may, through repentance and endurance, become uplifted by them and, through Christ's atonement and mercy, become one with Them. Therefore, you become perfected in Him as you release your sins to Him, and He assumes responsibility for them. His expression of love for His children has no bounds, no end, and is one of His greatest and most precious gifts to you all. It is expressed freely and demands nothing in return. He would like you to understand His love, accept it, and learn to express it as freely as He does. Since His love is the source of your love, the degree to which you accept love is the degree to which you are limited in expressing it to others. Becoming one with God means learning to allow your body and mind to be filled completely with His love. Only then will you be able to express it as He does, with complete power and authority.

"All humans are extensions of God's love. The extent or degree to which you accept and integrate this love into the fabric of your life, your thoughts, and your actions is the extent to which you can relate to others with love and harmony. The more you understand and live this concept, the greater will be your harmony with God's plans for you.

"As humans," John continued, "your biggest problem lies in the fact that you insist on believing that each person is an individual being who is completely separate from everything or everyone. This thinking isolates you from one another, and from God and His love. It not only diminishes you, but it diminishes your individual abilities. Accepting Christ includes accepting His love, His way of life, His ordinances, and His way to perfection. It does not mean that you can accept your own belief systems as the way of returning to Him. Accepting Christ is accepting His love and, in turn, expressing it to others.

"If you can but grasp the idea that you are an extension of God's love, then you can accept the concept that you are one with Him, that you are lifted up by Him in the perfection of His mercy. You will then delight in all the charitable outflows from Him, which will enhance your life immeasurably.

"This is not just a love that you should accept when you are in great need. It is a love that must become an integral and personal part of each moment of every day. It must become such a part of you that you feel its presence deep within your soul. It must become such a part of you that you would not feel whole without it.

"Love is not the simple emotion you may have been led to believe it is, although some very deep and powerful emotions are associated with it. Love is very complex in that it is comprised of many unifying, cohesive elements or traits. God expresses each of these elements as part of His love for you, and although they are separate elements, they, in their entirety, flow from God as love. Each of the unifying elements of love has an opposing, disunifying, or destructive element as its counterpart. Love is the basic force of life and unity. Hate and fear are the basic forces of destruction and disunity.

"The elements of both love and hate are empowered by the degree of their expression. Whichever element you choose to express at any given moment, as well as the degree of empowerment you assign it, will determine the consequence you reap. As I said, the elements of both forces always are held in perfect and delicate balance, and the continued expression of them forms the intentions that govern your life. You then become what your ruling affection is: good or evil, love or hate, unity or disunity, service-centered or self-centered.

"These," John said, "are some of the elements of unity: love, charity, kindness, compassion, consideration, gentleness, forgiveness, gratitude, humility, tenderness, honesty, non-prejudice, tolerance, truthfulness, morality, repentance, hope, faith, and patience.

"The elements of disunity include hate, anger, greed, dishonesty, intolerance, lying, prejudice, unforgiveness, unrepentance, hostility, envy, doubt, immorality, pride, contention, selfishness, and cruelty.

"There are many other elements from which to choose. Search them out and add them to your own list.[1]

"The expression of the elements of love and unity has the blessing of reaping life, abundance, joy, happiness, contentment, peace, innocence, confidence, strength, serenity, health, light, freedom, and harmony.

"The expression of the elements of hate and disunity has the curse of producing death, unhappiness, misery, illness, discontent, weakness, bondage, turmoil, destruction, poverty, fear, guilt, worry, stupidity, darkness, pain, and enslavement.

"It is not sufficient to simply avoid the elements of hate and disunity," John cautioned. "You also must express the components of unity and love. The thrust of your expression should always be away from disunity and toward unity, or away from the elements of hate and toward love.

"The nature of your personality is defined by certain characteristics and traits. These identify who you are and how you live your life. It is by these that you will ultimately be judged: opinions, appetites, attitudes, fixations, habits, desires, wants, beliefs, talents, ambitions, intentions, thoughts, compulsions, states-of-mind, morals, ethics, and standards.

"You must always strive to perfect each of these characteristics, progressing from being destructive toward being loving and expressing unity. Shifting and changing your traits and characteristics from the category of disunity to unity is probably one of the most difficult tasks you can ever undertake. The preservation of your agency and the agency of others should also be a major consideration. Anything that diminishes anyone's agency to any degree increases enslavement and dependency on something or someone other than you.

"The nature of mans personality is defined by the following characteristics and traits. They identify what he is and how he lives his life. It is by them that he is ultimately judged:

Opinions, appetites, attitudes, fixations, habits, desires, wants, beliefs, talents, ambitions, intentions, thoughts, compulsions, morals, ethics, and standards.

"You must always strive to perfect each of these elements and characteristics, progressing from being destructive towards love and unity.

"The product or result of perfecting your characteristics," John explained, "is unity, joy, happiness, health, peace, contentment, spiritual growth, and a feeling of being at one with God, others, and the universe, of being in harmony with His purpose and mission for you. As you begin to express these characteristics in a more loving manner, more abundantly, and in greater detail, you will progress toward an existence where an increasing amount of power and dominion will be given to you. You will expand your awareness outwardly and inwardly, and will learn from firsthand experience that you are, indeed, connected to all others and to God, spiritually and mentally. *You are never alone.* The constant presence and influence of angels or guides, as well as the presence of Satan and his hordes, maintains the delicate balance that provides you with one of the most precious gifts of all; agency. What you do with this agency, good or evil, productive or counter-productive—affects the whole of humankind. Love magnifies love, and hate magnifies hate.

"Here are a few thoughts about love that you would do well to memorize and live by," he continued. "Love is complete only when you understand and learn to express and integrate all of its elements into your daily life. Only then will your life be made whole, on target with your spiritual goals, and completely aligned with God and His purpose and mission for you.

"The expression of love, reflected in service to and compassion for others, is the only way to become completely integrated and at one with all.

"Love is the unifying force and energy of all life in the universe. It is the binding power of all physical matter, which is one of the expressions of God's love.

"No illness, disease, or malfunction of the body or mind can exist in an environment of complete, pure, and unconditional love. And that environment can only be created when all the elements of disunity and hatred have been purged through the forgiveness and repentance process, and all of the elements of love have been embraced. Elements of love and hate cannot coexist. It is impossible to express an element of love and one of hate at the same time.

"Part of your responsibility to the laws of love is to learn the laws of health," John went on. "The basic law of health is this: allow nothing to enter your mind or body that will affect you in an adverse or destructive way. Only allow those things into your mind and body that are life-giving or growth-producing.

"A great many illnesses are the result of the past or present expression of the elements of disunity and hate, on a conscious or subconscious level, by yourself or by someone you accept as an authority figure. This includes all traumatic experiences, whether involving only you or co-created with others. The elements of hate produce an energy field within you that is counter to the force of life. Modern psychology agrees that mental and emotional stress creates illness. Each unresolved element of hate creates an individual force field within you that affects the life force of all cells, tissues, organs, and systems within the body. When enough of these counter-to-life forces exist within you, they create illness—and eventually death. It is up to you to choose which force to embrace: one for life, the other for destruction and death.

"And so, to answer your question," John said, "you exist, in part, to help raise the level of love and spiritual awareness of all humanity. In so doing, your love is magnified.

"You exist to earn the great privilege of having an eternal body, at one with spirit and God, in physical form.

"You exist to become aligned and unified, in love, with all who are willing to make the effort to know and become one with God in purpose.

"Your physical form or body naturally resists the input from its spirit and the Holy Ghost. Your body tends to satisfy its own physical wants and needs before its spiritual needs. This may be in direct conflict to your spiritual purpose and growth.

"When perfect alignment occurs, and the elements of hate and disunity are completely dispelled, and the elements of love are completely embraced, then you will be well on your way to the perfection that God has commanded of you. Perfect alignment exists only when all the elements of love are continuously, freely, and joyously expressed.

"A complete, pure field of unconditional love can exist only when all the elements of hate and disunity have been supplanted by all the elements of unity and love.

"You must accept and bless everyone for the magnificent entities they truly are, and you must bless their efforts to create themselves in the way that they desire to fulfill their own agenda in this creation.

"Humanity's entire existence is explained by a comprehensive understanding of the relationship between humans, their spirits, and God," he continued. "You cannot gain a complete picture of this relationship without an understanding of the destructive elements of hate and disunity, and the important role they play in your life. There must be an opposition in all things, or growth would be impossible. There could be no love if there were no hate because there would be no reference point. Without reference points, this would be a very nondescript world: no happiness or sadness, no love or hate. In fact, without love *and* hate, humanity could not exist.

"Perhaps when most of humanity has learned to embrace and express unity and love to the fullest extent, and to reject the destructive forces of disunity and hate, more will be revealed. Every nation has access to scriptures or religious writings that teach of love and the unity of all humankind. Time is getting extremely short for humans, and only those who have learned to express the elements of love to

God and others, regardless of nationality, status, race, creed, or any other characteristic, will have the opportunity to truly live with God and inherit all that He has. Those who live by belief systems that are not based on God's love, laws, and commandments will be relegated to one of the lesser kingdoms. The impetus of humankind's unethical, immoral, and 'anything-goes' behavior is carrying humans to a sure physical and spiritual destruction unless these attitudes can somehow be reversed. *There is very little time left for humans to change the direction of their spiritual growth.*

"When humans can completely place their trust in the wisdom and intelligence of God and not rely on their own imperfect wisdom and knowledge, they will be well on their way to again residing with God," John concluded.

This was almost more than I could handle. I thought of all the religions in the world that claim their beliefs are the only way to salvation, yet preach disunity, hate, and prejudice. They often target another denomination or a segment of society for persecution. I wondered what would happen if all those religions renounced their self-serving traditions, their self-righteousness, their selfish aims, their need to obtain money and power at the expense of others and started living and teaching the true elements of unity and love. What a different world this would be.

CHAPTER FOUR

Charity

"It would now be my pleasure to discuss the concept of charity," John continued. "But first, let me quote Paul's first letter to the Corinthians, Chapter 13:

Though I speak with the tongues of men and of angels, and have not charity, I am become as sounding brass, or a tinkling cymbal.

And though I have the gift of prophecy, and understand all mysteries, and all knowledge; and though I have all faith, so that I could remove mountains, and have not charity, I am nothing.

And though I bestow all my goods to feed the poor, and though I give my body to be burned, and have not charity, it profiteth me nothing.

Charity suffereth long, and is kind; charity envieth not; charity vaunteth not itself, is not puffed up. Doth not behave itself unseemly, seeketh not her own, is not easily provoked, thinketh no evil;

Rejoiceth not in iniquity, but rejoiceth in the truth; Beareth all things, believeth all things, hopeth all things, endureth all things.

Charity never faileth: but whether there be prophecies, they shall fail; whether there be tongues, they shall cease; whether there be knowledge, it shall pass away.

For we know in part, and we prophesy in part. But when that which is perfect is come, then that which is in part shall be done away.

When I was a child, I spake as a child, I understood as a child, thought as a child; but when I became a man, I put away childish things.

For now we see through a glass, darkly; but then face to face: now I know in part; but then shall I know even as also I am known.

And now abideth faith, hope, charity, these three; but the greatest of these is charity.

"Charity is a two-fold concept," John explained. "First, you must learn to accept charity from Christ; second, you must learn to express it to others with complete, unconditional love.

"You can express generosity by giving to others, but unless you give with pure intent of heart, with unconditional love, and without hope of recompense, it isn't charity.

"Consider yourself a vessel of the Lord, perhaps like a water glass. If you accept just a drop of His charity, then that is the amount you will be able to express to others. If you accept a quarter-full glass of charity, then you may express that amount to others. You cannot express that which you don't have or refuse to accept. God and Christ are the source of all love and charity. You can use and express only as much as you have accepted from them. Christ's atonement is part of the charity He extends to you. This atonement, like charity and love, is not forced on you. You must make the choice and expend the effort to accept the atonement willingly or it will be of no value to you.

"You would do well to study the atonement and learn what it has to offer you. Without it, you would be subject to the law of justice only, and would be completely lost.

"There are several steps to accepting charity:

1. "You must gain all the knowledge you can about charity.
2. "You must study the concept of humility and become humble.

3. "You must learn to express love unconditionally.
4. "You must be completely obedient to all of God's laws and commandments, and when you are disobedient, you must repent through baptism and receive the Holy Ghost by one having authority to do so.
5. "You must always give thanks through prayer for who you are.
6. "As you learn to accept charity, you must learn to express it; as you express it, you magnify it in your own life.

"All charity flows from Christ in many forms. Everything you have in this world, spiritually and physically, is part of Christ's charity. The atonement and charity are two of the most cherished gifts from Him. Other gifts include love, talents, intelligence, wisdom, and knowledge.

"You can know nothing of truth except through the charity of Jesus Christ. Innocence, which is the result of repentance and the willingness to be led by Christ and not by yourself or others, is another exceptional gift. Once you accept that nothing in this world of any eternal value originates with you, but, in truth, flows from God and Christ as charity, you are well on your way to exceptional spiritual growth. Charity is the pure love of Jesus Christ!

"I think I will say no more on charity at this time," John concluded. "What else would you like to know?"

CHAPTER FIVE

On Thought

I had often wondered what constituted thought, so I decided to make that my next question.

"Just what is 'thought?'" I asked.

"Now, that's a thoughtful question," John chuckled. "Your mind uses the combined knowledge of spirit and body along with the promptings of those spirits whom some call guardian angels, or guides, assigned to help you in this life. As much as you might not want to admit it, your perception of good and evil is affected by the input from Satan's horde of evil angels. Your thoughts come from both physical experiences that begin at birth and extend to the present, and spiritual memories that extend backward in time to infinity. The mind is that intelligence that utilizes knowledge from both the spiritual and physical worlds but seems to have expression only in the physical. Your thoughts and experiences are recorded in both the physical and spiritual brains. Otherwise, all life memories would be erased upon death, and life would be meaningless and useless to you.

"The mind could be further described as the 'I am,' or the intelligent awareness that makes the statement, 'I exist.' Everything that exists in both the physical and spiritual realms is an extension or expression of the processing of thought, and of all sensory and psychic information, by both the physical and spiritual brains. Therefore, everything that appears to exist does so only as *your* creation, for *you*, in *your* mind. This does not mean that things don't exist outside your mind, but rather that your awareness of the existence of things is a creation of your brain based on your past experiences, sensory input, and thoughts. Without your intellect and your awareness, nothing could exist for you.

"Everything you do in this life is preceded by thought. All your beliefs are the result of judgments you have made based on sensory input and thought processes. Since no one else controls your thinking, you are completely responsible for what you have created yourself to be. What you accept as reality is, indeed, reality for you. If your reality included your being able to walk on water, then you could do so. Your limitations are set by the judgments of your thoughts and sensory input. Rejudge your thoughts, and you change your reality.

"Unlimited thinking opens the limitless possibilities of the mind's potential," John continued. "The mind is the most powerful tool humans have. 'As he thought in his heart, so is he' (Prov. 23:7). 'All things are possible to him that believeth' (Mark 9:23). These biblical teachings are intended to expand your abilities, if you will but grasp the concept that nothing is impossible."

"Why does there appear to be such a discrepancy between science and religion?" I asked.

"Because humans do not comprehend these two in their proper perspective," he replied. "Science is only humanity's feeble attempt to understand, measure, explain, and experiment with God's creation, trying to comprehend His physical environment. In the final analysis, there will be no discrepancy whatsoever. Humans are incapable of grasping the whole of God's creation. Therefore, all their measuring and theorizing will never be complete until God reveals His entire creation."

We were circling the lake by this time, watching an occasional trout disturb the mirror-like surface. I can't remember ever feeling such peace and tranquility.

"This has been such an extraordinary morning for me," I sighed. "It would be nice if times like these could last forever. But you've given me so much to think about that I'm not sure I'll be able to remember it all!"

"Oh, I'm sure that when the time comes for you to put it all on paper, it will all come back to you," John said reassuringly. "Do you have anything else you would like clarified?"

"Many things," I replied.

CHAPTER SIX

On Churches

"Is there really a church or religion on the earth today that follows the precepts of love and that has the true authority to act in the name of Jesus Christ?" I asked.

"Yes, there is!" John declared. "But since it is comprised of ordinary men, women, and children, even this church is found wanting in the areas of unity and love. I will not reveal its name, because the experiences you gain as you search for it are necessary for your spiritual growth. As with all life experiences, the ones that have the most value are those gained by trial and error, and by searching. And, if I were I to tell you the name of this church, there is a good possibility that you and others would not embrace all its concepts and would soon reject it.

"The seeds of faith must be planted in deep, rich soil—the soil of experience and desire—or they will wither and die. The truth is that most people do not have the sustaining desire necessary to rise above worldly distractions, such as the need for possessions and attachments, and to maintain the level of spiritual activity and sacrifice required by God. Your ultimate testimony of the rightness and truthfulness of the church's teachings depend, to a large extent, on the experience of the search. You will know it when you find it. Christ and God are the same yesterday, today, and forever, so study how He organized His church when He was on earth.

"When you find Christ's true church it isn't the *people* within the church who are important, it is the *truth of the principles* that make up the church's body of knowledge. The church members are just like you. They, too, are searching and growing, and they may not be capable of living all the elements of unity and love as they should. All churches have a place in this world. Every man, woman, and child are at a different level of growth, and some are just not ready to give up the things they must in order to belong to Christ's true church. His church is one of sacrifice, where the members must be willing to give up the things of the world and embrace the things of the spirit.

"Humans not only like to hold on to their physical attachments, but also to the prejudices and beliefs that delude them into thinking they have been elevated above others. They like the idea of being superior to others of different religions, sects, races, statuses, and so on. Most people in this life are content to live out their lives in the shadow of the traditions of their parents. They don't want to rock the boat or cause a rift in the family. Their curiosity is seldom sufficient to investigate the possibility that any other church or religion could offer them more than they already have. Most believe what their ecclesiastical leaders teach them, and they don't make the effort to study the scriptures, pray, or think for themselves. They are content to accept the teachings of their pastors or priests as truth and have been taught never to question pastoral or priestly authority.

"However, the ultimate responsibility for your spiritual education and growth lies only with *you*, not with your parents, society, or ecclesiastical leaders," John said. "To grow spiritually, you must always question, and you must compare human teachings to the scriptures. When there appears to be a discrepancy, you must elect to believe the scriptures. Pray without predetermined convictions and with deep meditation, and the Holy Spirit will manifest the truth to you. Pray with sincerity and an open mind. Pray with power. Pray with the knowledge that God will answer."

CHAPTER SEVEN

On Beliefs

"How can all the churches and religions of the world believe with such conviction that theirs is the only true church on earth?" I asked.

"Before you can understand this, you must comprehend what a belief is and from where it comes," John explained. "A belief is a judgment that you have made about the authoritativeness, acceptability, and truth of a thought, idea, or information that you have received or generated. It is a concept or idea in which you have put your faith and on which you base your actions. The authenticity you have assigned to it determines whether you act on it or not. The more truth or authenticity you assign to a belief, the more likely you are to live by and act within the confines of that belief. All your actions, and many of your thoughts, have their roots in the beliefs you have established. Every belief you adopt, or form draws to it the experiences and evidence necessary to reinforce, satisfy, and sustain the needs generated by the belief.

"One of the greatest sins in this world is that humans follow the traditions of their parents. (Mark 7:5-9) These traditions are nothing more than beliefs and belief systems that have been passed on from family to family.

"There will never be a better time than now for everyone on earth to closely examine all their beliefs—not only religious beliefs, but all beliefs by which they live," John stated. "Beliefs that are not based on the elements of love and the knowledge found in the scriptures, and which do not produce a cleansing of the mind and body from the elements of disunity and hate, must be excised."

He continued: "The key to living your life in harmony with God's purpose lies in the deep reaches of the thought process, which you must learn to completely control. Any deliberate act is always preceded by thought. Every judgment leading to a belief is preceded by thought. You must think with intelligence, knowledge, and wisdom. Examine every thought for validity and truth. This will go a long way in helping you to avoid those beliefs not founded in eternal truth. Every limit you assign to yourself is preceded by a thought or an acceptance of someone else's thought. Limits are mostly self-containing, confining, and destructive to spiritual growth.

"The elements of unity and love are expansive toward limitlessness and toward unrestricted abilities. Conversely, the elements of disunity and hate are limiting, restrictive, and ultimately destructive. They lead to curtailed abilities, misery, sadness, illness, loss of hope, and ultimately to both spiritual and physical death.

"Remember this: all truth is eternal and can stand alone. Therefore, only beliefs founded on the principals of eternal truth needn't be changed or purged. All others should be examined very closely.

"And so," John said, "the beliefs in most churches are merely the adoption of the traditions of parents, teachers, ecclesiastical leaders, and peers. Few have the courage or make the time to discover truth for themselves. They just adopt what others convince them is the truth. They are followers of their church leaders, not necessarily of Christ. They pray with prejudice to find the truth.

"Praying with prejudice means that you have made up your mind before hand as to the truthfulness or untruthfulness of a teaching, and then you pray to know the truth. What you actually are doing is praying in vain or praying for confirmation of your beliefs. Praying with an open mind and a sincere desire to know is to put aside all preconceived notions or judgments. This allows the Holy Spirit to manifest truth to you.

"To ask spiritual leaders about the truth of their religions serves no purpose. This only encourages you to live your life based on the testimony of others and will profit you nothing. Most people do not take the time to study and learn for themselves. Most ecclesiastical leaders fear the loss of their positions and income, so their answers tend to perpetuate their own religions and positions. To find the truth takes time, work, a lot of searching, prayer, and a great deal of commitment.

"Your entire life here on earth should be lived to prepare you for the next stage of existence that you call 'death.' Your spiritual growth, your knowledge, your intelligence, your wisdom, your service to others, your repentance, and the amount of love you have accepted and express here will all determine the stage of growth at which you will begin your next period of progression. Those who have developed all the elements of love to the greatest degree will have a much greater advantage than those who haven't. Many will begin the search; some will make the discovery; but very few will remain committed to the find," he said. "However, those who do remain committed will have the greatest advantage and will enjoy the greatest spiritual growth.

"Death does not change a personality. The same memories, habits, tendencies, beliefs, attitudes, prejudices, appetites, and desires will follow you into death, or your next stage of progression. If you die with hate and unforgiveness in your heart, those elements will remain with you in death. The only thing that will really change is that you will no longer have a body until after the resurrection.

"This life, then, is a preparation for the next step in spiritual growth. Are you ready for it?" John asked.

This was heavy stuff. I was a little sorry I had asked my question. Now I felt like I had an obligation to follow through and see if I could find this church that he said existed.

"So, where do I begin this search?" I asked.

"Wherever you want," he laughed. "It might be a good idea to approach it thoughtfully and prayerfully. Make a detailed plan of action, structure your time, and follow through."

We had circumnavigated the lake by this time and were beginning the ascent back up the trail from which we had come. We paused for a few minutes to look over the scenery. The peaks still had a goodly amount of snow, but that which had melted had produced some delightful waterfalls. It was, in its entirety, awesome.

As we proceeded up the trail, I wondered what I should ask next. I knew this day couldn't last forever, but I wanted to stave off its ending as long as I could. After some thought, I posed my next question.

CHAPTER EIGHT

On Faith

I had often wondered about faith. Why were we not able to do the things that the scriptures indicated we could? We should be able to move mountains or trees, raise the dead, heal the sick, walk on water, and do all the other things Christ did when He was on earth. "Verily, verily, I say unto you, He that believeth on me, the works that I do shall he do also; and greater works than these shall he do; because I go unto my Father" (John 14:12).

"What is faith, and what are the laws that govern it?" I asked.

"That's another thoughtful question," John replied. "Faith is not some abstract notion that is usable only by the prophets, as some people might believe. It is the principle and power behind all action. Faith is an element of love, and therefore must be used righteously and with thankfulness. It is the power by which all things exist, by which all things are created, and by which all things are accomplished.'

"Faith is comprised of the elements of hope, worthiness, expectance, belief, and especially knowledge. Without these five elements, there can be no exercise of faith. The stronger your hope, expectance, feeling of worthiness, and belief, and the more truth, authority, and authenticity you assign to your knowledge, the surer you can be that its application will bear fruit. The use of knowledge for any creation or production is faith in action. God has perfect knowledge, belief, hope, and expectation; therefore, the exercising of His faith is perfect. He speaks, and everything obeys His command.

"As you increase and become sure of your knowledge, you also increase the strength of your conviction, your hope, and your belief. The more truth and authenticity you assign to your knowledge and belief, the greater will be your ability to exercise faith. The surer you are of the truthfulness of your knowledge, the less doubt you will have in your ability to use it. Faith cannot be exercised in a field of doubt or fear.

"Always increase your knowledge but be careful of the truth and authenticity you assign to it. Just because someone else has assigned truth to some piece of knowledge does not mean that it can stand alone as truth in the eternities. All of God's knowledge is true; not all of humanity's is. By increasing true knowledge, you will find that acting on it with assurance will expand your ability to achieve. This is faith in action. If you know that something can be done, or has been done, then all that remains is to gain the knowledge and expertise required, and you can duplicate it. Everyone knows that buildings can be constructed; with the right expertise, you, too, can build one. The knowledge that something can be done goes a long way toward increasing your faith. To develop your faith, you must first acquire knowledge and expertise—and then use them. Simply gaining knowledge cannot develop faith. You must *act* on knowledge.

"Another way to describe faith is this: it is the action resulting from the expression of the belief that your knowledge, worthiness, hope, and expectation are sufficient for the task required of them," John said. "Faith is magnified if it is expressed in an environment of pure love."

CHAPTER NINE

On Success

For many years I had wondered why some people were successful, but others never seemed to get anywhere. Was it because of fate? Or were there some elements or secrets that successful people used that could help anyone to become successful?

I am not a great proponent of fate. I believe that we all create the lives we choose to live, and that we attract to us those experiences dictated by the beliefs we adopt as we go through this life.

"Why is it that some individuals seem to have all the luck, while others live in abject poverty?" I asked. "Why do some people have it all while others, regardless of how hard they try, never seem to get beyond the very basics of life?"

"This is a complicated question, and the answer lies in your beliefs and belief systems," John replied. "Your Savior said, 'If thou canst believe, all things are possible to him that believeth' (Mark 9:23). The question then becomes: how do you change your beliefs enough to make things happen? The more strongly you believe in something, the surer you can be that your efforts will bear fruit. Keep in mind that these beliefs must be seated in knowledge based on truth. The answer to making things happen lies in empowerment.

"Every word in every language on earth is assigned a certain amount of power by each individual who speaks that language. Some words have more power than others for an individual. The word 'war' has much more power and meaning for one who has seen combat than for one who hasn't. The word 'miracle' has more meaning for a Christian who has witnessed one than for an atheist who hasn't. People assign a predetermined amount of power to the words they use and may differ considerably from individual to individual and from situation to situation. You assign power to sentences, paragraphs, chapters, even to whole books. The power you assign to anything is based on the judgment you make on the viability, authenticity, authority, and truth of the concept in question. If you could assign complete truth to and empower the concepts of levitation, teleportation, walking on water, or any other number of things, you could do those things now. To completely validate any idea or belief will differ from one person to another. The concept of wealth, whether spiritual or monetary, will never work for you until you learn to completely empower the concept.

"The art of empowerment will come more easily for some than for others. Empowerment is the process by which you come to realize that you *know*, and that you know you *can*. It is the act of assigning absolute viability, truth, authority, and authenticity to an idea, concept, or thought. When you *know* something is true, you can act on it with a sure knowledge that your actions will bear fruit. If any doubt or fear creeps in, it will not happen. If you believe—unwaveringly, with absolute faith, without a doubt, having no fear—then anything is possible. Nevertheless, all things must be done in a field of pure love, without intending to hurt or debase anyone, or to elevate yourself above others. Otherwise, the process will only bring pain, misery, and destruction upon yourself. The empowerment process is the building of faith.

"The process of assigning absolute viability, truth, authority, and authenticity to a concept is not easy," John continued. "I listened intently as he explained the natural sequence of events." First, you must know with assurance that you want to empower it, and that it will not adversely affect anyone. Second, you must cast all doubt and fear out of your mind. Allowing any doubt or fear will nullify your endeavors. Third, you must believe that your idea is not only possible, but also that by your actions, it *will* happen. Fourth, you must convince your subconscious mind, your innate intelligence, and your spirit that your idea is what you desire above all else at that particular time and for that particular thing. This can be done by intense emotional repetition, by meditation, and by sincere prayer. It must be done in the silence of your mind, where no turmoil exists, and no distractions are present. To do this is seldom easy. It may take months or years of practice. And before you can do it, you must rid yourself of those elements of disunity that would bring doubt and fear into the equation. Your attitudes toward love and toward others may have to be brought into harmony with God's desires before your efforts will bear fruit. Not everyone will be able to use the more complex concepts and ideas.

"There is a natural pathway or sequence of events that leads from an idea to its achievement," John explained. "I give you this pathway in the hope that all who study it may benefit:

1. **Thought, idea, concept, or goal:** Thought is the source of all ideas and concepts. Since thought can be controlled to a great extent, humans have the capacity to productively create whatever they can conceive. Look around and see what thought has created: cars, houses, buildings of all kinds, computers, and so on. Every man-made object has its origin in thought and inspiration. Likewise, all spiritual growth also has its origin in thought and inspiration. Nothing can be denied those who have complete control over their thought processes.

2. **Desire and determination:** Once you know what you want to accomplish, or have an idea you wish to bring to fruition, you must create a burning desire and maintain a determination to see it through to completion. Without this drive and desire, little will happen.

3. **Intention and willingness:** After your drive has been created, you must have the intention and willingness to do

whatever it takes—within the confines of righteousness—to complete the project or accomplish your goal.

4. **Knowledge and expertise:** Hard as you may try, you cannot accomplish anything without the specialized knowledge or expertise required for your project. In some cases, more than just a working knowledge is required. For example, there have been many who had the information and ability, but didn't have the proof, such as a diploma; consequently, they were passed over for promotion. Even for inventors, proof of expertise is often a factor in determining success or failure.

5. **Plan of action:** A good, viable plan must be carefully and meticulously created with all the elements necessary to complete the project and reach your goal. Without a blueprint, a building cannot be built. A plan of action is a good blueprint. Don't be afraid to seek or accept help if necessary.

6. **Hope and belief:** Always maintain hope for the completion of your project, and belief in your idea and your ability to accomplish and achieve. The Bible states that all things are possible for him that believeth. (Mark 9:23)

7. **Faith:** Belief is the cornerstone, but faith is the power by which all things are accomplished. Faith is increased by doing, by continuously stretching your limitations and your imagination, and by finishing that which you have started. Not one of these eight steps could be accomplished without faith.

8. **Sustained effort:** This is the last step on the pathway to success. Make sure that all of these elements are bound with the strong bonds of morality and ethics. To accomplish a goal at the expense of another will hurt you far more than it hurts them, and, in the end, will only bring you pain and anguish. Whatsoever a man soweth that shall he also reep. (Galatains 6:7)

"Adherence to these steps," John continued, "yields achievement, accomplishment of physical and spiritual goals, and ultimate success. (Always emember, things physical are temporary and things spiritual are eternal.)

"In your search for achievement, negative elements such as distractions, doubts, and fears may creep in. Satan will make sure of this. He doesn't want anyone to be successful except at the expense of others. As these negative elements appear, take them one at a time, acknowledge them, but don't give in to them. Return your mind to the problems that created the doubts, solve them, and go on with the project. Don't become mired in distractions; instead, rise above them, and you will succeed.

On Health

I also had wondered many times why so many people seemed to be ill. Sickness was not just limited to the elderly; everyone seemed to be affected in one way or another. Some, it seemed, were affected all the time.

"Why is it that so many people seem to be sick all the time?" I asked. "What is health, and what can we do to maintain a perpetual state of good health and vitality?"

"There are so many facets to health that it would be impossible to discuss them all," John responded. "Every individual is unique. Their diets, genetics, exercise, states of mind, family backgrounds, habits, and much more play a part in their health. There are, however, some basic essentials.

"But before we can discuss health, you must understand what you are. Humans, like all life forms, are integrated energy systems comprised of physical, mental, emotional, and spiritual components. Each person vibrates or oscillates at a unique frequency. Within each person, every cell, tissue, organ, and system operates at a separate but harmonic frequency. When the frequencies of these elements exist within the parameters that produce health, then health exists. When, for whatever reason, there are counter-to-life frequencies, energies, or conditions—such as hatred, violence, unforgiveness, anger, fear, parasites, microorganisms, and so on—then illness will exist.[2]

"In the near future, there will be some major advancements in the treatment of health problems using electromagnetic frequency harmonic generation. Enveloping an ill person in a pulsating electromagnetic field that approximates the frequencies of his life energies will help to promote life and health. Dr. Royal Rife has already accomplished much work in this field, and more research is in progress. (See Dr. Royal Raymond Rife on the web)

"Since many illnesses are created by unresolved problems related to the elements of disunity, a new healing system will be developed which involves the excising of the elements of destruction through forgiveness therapy, neurolinguistic programming, hypnotherapy, and other related therapies.

"Health begins as a state of mind and body that embraces happiness, vitality, enthusiasm, stamina, exuberance, and a zest for living. If you exist in this state and continuously express love, wellness will result.

"In addition, when all cells, tissues, organs, and systems of the body function at optimum capacity and in complete harmony with one another and with the energies of life, wellness will result. Caring, sharing, repenting, and forgiving help to maintain the mind and body in a state of health. Perfect health cannot exist without surrendering and purging all the elements of hate and disunity, and without the perpetual expression of all of the elements of love and unity in all aspects of daily living.

"Both body and mind seek to maintain a stable internal environment as they continuously respond to internal and external stresses and activities. The internal environment will adapt to these stresses and activities—or to the lack of them. Muscles can be built with activity or can atrophy with disuse. The brain can increase its thinking capabilities with stimulation, or, again, it can atrophy with disuse. As the popular saying goes, 'Use it or lose it.'

"To express the elements of love and unity on a continuing basis, you must obey certain dietary, mental, and physical rules. Here are some guidelines that can help you immensely in caring for your health:

1. You must assume complete responsibility for your health. Most people believe that they can abuse their bodies and minds at will and their physicians will heal them. A good many physicians are not interested in health, only in illness. They can either point you in the direction of healing, or suppress the symptoms of illness. All healing takes place within the body and mind. Create the proper physical, mental, emotional, and spiritual environments, and healing will occur. Keep in mind that the spirit, or innate intelligence, is in control of healing, but it must have some help from its host.

2. Don't allow anything into your body or mind that is in opposition to your health or your own healing powers. This includes drugs, alcohol, caffeine, tobacco, toxins, or foods that cause allergic or sensitivity reactions. The mind is equally sensitive to degrading things. Everything you ingest with your five senses has an impact on your mind and influences your body: the violence you see on TV, pornography, computer games, and so on. The good things in this life also have an influence. Good books, uplifting art, and the like promote mental and spiritual growth, and health will follow.

3. Ingest as much live food as possible. Cooked foods, processed foods, frozen foods, and irradiated foods are mostly dead. Dead foods are devoid of life-enhancing enzymes and of many vitamins and minerals. Without enzymes, life would cease to exist. And, in today's environment, it is absolutely necessary for you to ingest good food supplements, since the farmlands have been depleted of many of the essential minerals and nutrients. Remember that most of the food industry is money-driven. Your health is of little concern to most in the industry.

4. Think in terms of health, not illness. Many humans create their illnesses by deliberately disobeying good health habits. Some enjoy ill health for the sympathy they receive—

the 'poor-me syndrome.' But self-pity has never helped anyone become or stay healthy.

5. Develop a progressive mental and physical exercise program that fits your age and your physical and mental condition. If you gradually increase the time and intensity of your workout, then you will feel more energetic, vital, and enthusiastic—regardless of your age. Your stamina will increase and your outlook on life will change for the better. Walking and swimming are great choices. For mental conditioning, write a book or your memoirs, engage in stimulating discussions, avoid arguments, learn chess, do crossword puzzles, and so on. If you have a heart condition, consult your physician before embarking on any exercise program.

6. Always remember that many illnesses come from the assimilation and expression of the elements of hate and disunity, by you or someone else. Health comes from the expression of love and unity. Stay in a repentant state at all times to be healthy.

7. Use moderation in all things. Don't overeat, not even on holidays. Don't watch too much TV; don't spend too much time reading. Be prudent in all that you do.

8. Include roughage in every meal. Strengthen your immune system by eating fresh, raw fruits and vegetables every day. They will replenish the enzymes necessary for life. And cleanse your bowels at least every six months with fruit juices. Again, be prudent, and don't go overboard. A three-day juice fast may work well for most people, but some may not be able to tolerate that.

9. Keep current on health research by subscribing to reputable health newsletters. The world is changing its views on health and wellness monthly.

10. Always be in harmony with God, nature, yourself, and others," John concluded.

CHAPTER ELEVEN

Prayer

We stopped about halfway to the pass and sat down on a grassy spot so that I could rest. I pondered my next question, knowing that my time with John was limited. "What, exactly, are prayer and meditation?" I asked.

"Prayer, supplication, and meditation are among the greatest powers on earth," he answered. "The very act of prayer is an indication of faith and an acknowledgment of the existence of God and Jesus Christ; in whose name you should perform all activities related to the Gospel and to salvation. The more you learn how to pray with true sincerity and faith, the more likely your prayers will be answered. Prayer is so important that many of your prophets have admonished you to pray continually: pray every morning, every noon, every night. Pray for health, pray for your herds, your crops, for wisdom and understanding. Pray for all needful things.

"Those of you who pray may have special times and places to approach God. Some successfully pray while they drive, walk, do the dishes, go fishing, or whatever. You need to select special times and places to pray. Make them where you can meditate and commune with God without interruption. You can receive the answers to many questions and problems in this manner.

"A special time for me to pray is during a church service. I believe that a person can draw closer to God during a church service than at any other time." I interrupted. "This is a good time to come clean before God and to ask forgiveness for the indiscretions of the week. It can be a time for deep reflection and meditation. It also can be a time for self-analysis, goal setting and deciding which areas of your life are most in need of improvement. Church service can be a quiet time that should be enjoyed and spent with your Father in Heaven."

"Most people don't pray often enough, nor with enough emotion, sincerity and desire." John continued. "The prophets and many Church leaders have spent a great deal of time on their knees and encourage you to do the same. Few people spend enough time on their knees. Some prophets have spent all day and long into the night, to gain a confirmation of the remission of their sins, and to attain a positive knowledge of God's forgiveness. Everyone needs to develop this kind of determination and faith.

"Whether or not your prayers are answered depends on several things," John said. "First, your Father in heaven treats you very much like you treat your own children when they ask you for a favor. You tend to withhold the requested item until it is earned. This is as it should be because God does the same thing to you. If you are in a state of repentance and obedience, you probably deserve the request you make in your prayers. Then, if your faith is sufficient, if your prayers are sincere and heartfelt, if the request is righteous and for your own good or for the good of another, God may grant it.

"God knows what is best for you, so not everything you request is freely given. Consequently, He may say no even when you are worthy of receiving a sought-after blessing. This can either build or destroy faith, depending on your attitude. If God withholds a blessing, you can accept His decision in good faith if you recognize that He knows what is best for you. It is when you continue to petition God after you have received a 'no' that you get into trouble. If you continually pester Him, you just may get the thing for which you asked—even when God knows that it is not in your best interests. Then you must go through the painful process of learning by experience. After the trial is over, you may not be in such a hurry to pester Him again when He has refused a petition."

John's words recalled an experience that taught my wife and me how essential it is to rely on the answers God gives us, and to have faith that things will turn out right.

"That reminds me of the time when Geri and I decided we needed another car," I said. "We had been married for about a year when I was transferred from Fort Huachuca, Arizona, to Fort Bliss, Texas. We felt that our old Buick was on its last legs, so we had decided to purchase a 'new' used car in either Tucson or Phoenix. We prayed the night before, and again on the morning we left, that we would find the car we should buy.

"Having searched the Tucson market without finding a car that was affordable and suitable, we decided to go on to Phoenix and look there. The day was as hot as a midsummer day in Arizona can be. We were suffering from the heat, and frustrated that we hadn't found a car in Tucson.

"The baby, who was just a few weeks old, also was hot and fussy, so we decided to see if we could leave him with his great-grandmother in Coolidge. She reluctantly agreed to watch him, but insisted that we be back before 2:00PM so she could attend a church meeting.

"It was now 11:00AM, and I received the strong impression that we should wait to buy a car. Time was running out, and Phoenix was an hour's drive away. We decided to go into Florence, just ten miles away, to get our old car inspected to expedite the title transfer. When we arrived, we found that the inspection mechanic had left for lunch a few minutes earlier and wouldn't be back for more than an hour.

"By this time the heat and our frustration had reached a peak. We called the café where the inspector normally ate lunch, but he wasn't there. Geri was very distraught by this time. She felt that there must be something more we could do to get things moving. But I felt that since we had prayed and put it into God's hands, everything that could be done had been done.

"Geri went off in a huff, the heat and frustration bearing down on her. She crossed the street to a variety store and wandered around for a few minutes. Then she also came to realize that God was trying to tell us, 'Not at this time.' She came back with a box of Cracker Jacks—a peace offering—and said, 'Let's go home.' I agreed. We went back to Coolidge, picked up our son, and returned to Fort Huachuca.

"Upon arriving at Fort Bliss, we found housing to be in scarce supply. Rentals were almost nonexistent, and the few that were available were very expensive. To stay together as a family, we had to purchase a house. Had we bought another car, we surely would have lost it. God, in His wisdom, had known what our monetary situation would be in Texas. By heeding His promptings, we saved ourselves a lot of misery. Our old car did survive the trip and gave us transportation for another two years."

John nodded his head. "It's not always easy to hear God, especially when aggravating circumstances overwhelm you. You can't hear the music for the noise. When you have difficulty hearing the answer to a prayer you can get yourself into trouble that could be prevented if you would just be calm, patient, and learn to listen.

"That's an important lesson from which everyone could learn," John continued. "You must learn to rely on His wisdom, power, justice, and mercy—without equivocation, and in true humility.

"Each of you possesses different elements and attitudes that may block the answers coming from God. Let me share some of these with you so that you can gain a greater understanding of the necessity of approaching your Heavenly Father in the proper manner:

1. **Love:** Love is so important that you must give its development top priority in your life. The magnitude of God's love for you is mostly incomprehensible to you humans. It is hard for you to understand how He can love all of you equally, even those who are disobedient and ebellious. To develop and elevate your love to the same level as God's love for you, especially when you have great evils perpetrated against you, is beyond your abilities. It is easy to love those who are sweet, kind, and loving to you. The true test comes when you are required to love your enemies. Here you must rely on God's power and wisdom to

help you to first, create the desire, then to take the actions necessary to help you love them. As you develop this love, through prayer, your efforts will be much more effective. This is only possible if you continue to express and increase your love for others. You cannot hoard your love like a miser and expect it to grow. Nor can you ignore it. But, if you develop and nurture your love, freely giving it to and accepting it from others, your prayers will take on new meaning and be more acceptable to God. Harboring hate or any destructive trait or element only harms you, not those against whom the hate is directed.

2. **Vain repetitions:** It is very difficult to pray day after day and not repeat yourself. But it is vanity that is mostly the problem, not repetition. *Webster's New World Dictionary* defines vanity as: '(1) Having no real value or significance, worthless, empty, idle, hollow, etc. (2) Without force or effect, futile, fruitless, unprofitable, unavailing, etc. (3) Having or showing an excessively high regard for oneself, looks, possessions, ability, etc.; indulging in or resulting from personal vanity; conceited. [Archaic] Lacking in sense; foolish.'

   "From this definition, it is not hard to understand why your Savior dislikes vain repetitions. Vanity is an enemy of humility. If your prayers are idle, hollow, empty, and have no force, God will not look upon them with any degree of interest. If you approach Him under the influence of any of the counterproductive traits, it is unlikely that He will heed your prayer. Before your prayers can be answered, vanity and the rest of the destructive traits must not be present.

3. **Emotional state:** Experience has shown that you are more apt to gain solace and comfort, and to receive answers to your prayers, when you are in the depths of despair or when some crisis exists in your life. When your emotions are deep and sincere, when your concern for others is at a peak, and especially when you believe you deserve that

for which you are asking, God is more likely to respond to your needs. He wants to help you, and He will—if you learn to approach Him in humility. Seldom will you receive His help when you feel you are unworthy or undeserving.

"The first step in making yourself worthy is sincere, daily repentance. Your supplication must be made with true emotion, never faked. You should be hopeful, have faith, and pray only for that which is necessary for your sustenance and what is needful for you and your loved ones' salvation and survival. God will hear your prayers and give you the challenges you need for growth and progress. Although He always knows what is best for you, He wants you to ask. This not only builds your faith, but also helps you realize how much you must depend on Him for everything in this life.

4. **Attitudes:** Humility, meekness, and hope are among the most important attitudes you must demonstrate when approaching God in prayer. The realization that God is involved in every aspect of your life is essential when you kneel before Him. If you pray not expecting to receive an answer, why bother? This expectation is called 'hope,' and hope must be followed by faith. When you kneel before God, and you believe you are worthy, your expectations have a greater chance of being realized—unless they may be harmful to your growth and progress. Other attitudes that are equally important are those of service, love, and charity. If you strive to develop these positive attitudes, your Father in heaven will be more likely to hear and answer your prayers.

5. **Desire:** If your desires are righteous and intense, God is more likely to answer your prayers. If you offer up an apathetic supplication, you have little hope of having it answered; but generating a false intensity is vain. Creating a genuinely intense desire for something that is good, righteous, and necessary for your growth and progress is not easy. If you are involved in conquering a destructive trait,

and you approach God in a lackadaisical manner with no depth of feeling, He will see your insincerity. Therefore, He may not grant you the strength or challenges you need to overcome the trait. On the other hand, if you can convince Him that you are really serious about your endeavor by your intensity and persistence, then He will be more likely to help you conquer the trait. God can look into your heart and see when you're sincere. If your petition is truly your desire, He will give accordingly. When you pray day after day for the same blessings and form no plan of action to gain them, He knows that you are not really serious. Most people are comfortable with their lifestyles and are not likely to change unless something drastic comes along to promote the change. If you pray and expect God to do it all, you are sure to be disappointed. How true the old saying is: 'Pray as if everything depends on God, then act as if everything depends on you.' God will help you only when you put forth every possible effort required to obtain the blessings you seek. ' If you were God, would you answer the pleas of those who constantly asked you to help the needy and the widows—especially when the requesters had the means to give assistance themselves? But if they asked you to help them find ways that they themselves could give aid and sustenance, you would be most happy to give them the ideas and the strength for this accomplishment.

"When you pray, you must look into your heart and determine whether your desires are sincere and what you seek is needful. Do not pray for God to help the widows, the needy, the orphans, and so on. Instead, pray that *you* can find a way to help—not for your own glory, but in secret, with a sincere desire to help, with charity in your heart. God will then provide the ways and means to make the plans you formulate come to fruition.

6. **Enthusiasm:** God answers your prayers with the same enthusiasm you use when you approach Him. If your prayers lack vigor, how can you expect God to be enthusi-

astic about answering? When you pray with intensity, then strive with equal zeal to accomplish that for which you have prayed, God will help you with that same enthusiasm. Therefore, there is nothing you cannot accomplish. If you could just learn to approach your whole life with enthusiasm, it would soon become second nature to pray in the same manner, and indeed your prayers would not be in vain.

7. **Anger:** When you are angry, hurt, or resentful, you are deeply in need of communication with your Father in heaven. But it is counterproductive to approach Him with these negative emotions. You need to take a few moments and meditate. Think of God and His great mercy, His tolerance for your deficiencies and aberrations. Realize that it is Satan who is behind your negative feelings. Then, when you have calmed down, when humility and peace reign, you can approach your Father in heaven, and He will be more likely to hear your pleas.

   "Anger is learned in early childhood as a response to negative stimuli. It is one of the most violent emotions and can be extremely destructive to relationships. Anger is a mask behind which you can hide your true emotions and vulnerabilities. You can use it to protect yourself from being hurt, or to bend others to your will. Anger is a satanic weapon used to control and dominate others. Anger is always a choice. Realizing this is the secret to overcoming its influence in your life. Make the choice to not be angry and you have control over it.

8. **Greed:** Greed is a real enemy to prayer. God knows your true personality, and if you are greedy and selfish, then you are unlikely to receive anything you ask for—except the strength to overcome your greed and to be forgiven. If you continually seek money or power, or if gaining worldly possessions is your primary goal in life, then you are indeed in the bondage of sin. Your prayers are likely to fall on deaf ears unless you are asking for help to over-

come this destructive trait. If you are seeking wealth in righteousness with the intent of helping others, then God may hear your prayers and bless you accordingly. Giving is the secret to overcoming greed. With joy you must give of your love, time, substance, and talents. Always be willing to help those who are less fortunate than you. God will then answer your prayers in every way He can. When you get involved in helping others, your own problems diminish and you become healthier and happier.

9. **Goals:** Your goals set the theme for many of your prayers. God will help you when your goals are things that are eternal in nature, such as perfecting your body, mind, and spirit. To set your sights on attaining worldly possessions may not elicit a favorable response. Setting and accomplishing ideals through prayer is essential to your salvation and exaltation. However, your goals must be in harmony with God's plans for your eternal progress toward perfection. Your greatest accomplishments come as the result of setting and attaining goals. You should set daily goals that will stretch the limits of your capabilities for that day. Do the same thing weekly and monthly. Setting righteous short- and long-term goals not only will bring you closer to God, but also will challenge your abilities and talents. Goals are the meat of accomplishment. Without them, you ride aimlessly on a sea of procrastination, waiting for fate to deal you a better hand, waiting for your ship to come in, waiting for someone to drop that great deal in your lap. Goals will help you buy that ship, and you can deal yourselves whatever hand it takes to make you prosperous in the eyes of God. All you must do, with the help of the Lord, is set and achieve those objectives that are oriented toward growth and progress."

After John fell silent, we sat there on the grass in companionable silence for a while. Then I remembered an important incident of answered prayer in my own life.

"John, I want to share this with you," I said. "When Geri and I were living in Fort Huachuca, Arizona, early in our marriage, we moved from an apartment about 20 miles from the Fort to a less-expensive mobile home that was much closer to work.

"Our move came near the end of the month and, like most military families, we were dead broke. The gauge on our old gas-guzzling Buick registered almost empty—and when the indicator reached empty, it meant there really wasn't any gas left.

"We prayed that there would be enough gasoline to make the move. We then proceeded to make three trips, moving all of our household goods with full confidence that we would have enough fuel. We made the last two trips with the indicator right on 'empty.' In fact, we traveled at least one hundred miles that way.

"After the move, we decided to haul some full garbage cans to the dump, still believing that the Lord was continuing to answer our prayers. As we started for the dump, a friend who was helping us move lost his faith and said, 'Pull into the nearest gas station—my faith has just run out!' Our faith had never faltered, and the Lord blessed us accordingly.

"There have been many such faith-building events in my life," I said. "I know that when I am living in harmony with God's will and in a repentant state, the prayers I offer in humility will be answered if they are best for my growth and well-being."

CHAPTER TWELVE

Meditation

John paused for a few moments in appreciation of my story. Then he continued:

"You asked about both prayer and meditation. You can and should meditate about the many important things in life, but you should never confuse meditation with fantasizing. The fantasies, many of you practice at times, should be controlled, and used only for your growth toward perfection. Sexual and other negative fantasies should be entirely avoided as they are destructive to your growth and often become an acceptable part of your real lives. They can destroy relationships just as surely as actions. They leave you with not only a need for bigger and better fantasies but actions that match them. 'For as he thinketh in his heart, so is he.' (Proverbs 23:7) or to paraphrase, as a man thinks in his heart, he is sure to become. Also, 'For where your treasure is, there will your heart be also.' (Matthew 6:21)

"Meditating is one of the most powerful forces on earth. Every human accomplishment has been planned for in men's minds. It is through the spirit of Christ that man receives all righteous thoughts, ideas, and inventions. Nothing of any value will come from man unless it is first studied out in his mind. Anything you want to do can be accomplished if it is desired with your whole heart; reflected on and acted upon. Thought is the precursor to success in every endeavor. Every achievement depends on several things. (See the chapter on success)

"Once the desire has jelled and the planning has been completed, success is almost guaranteed. By thought and concentration—by meditation—you must plan all your accomplishments, whether they are great or small, physical, or spiritual. These thoughts and plans are the *spiritual* creation of that which you wish to accomplish. The actual achievement is the *temporal* creation. If you have a strong desire to do something, whether it be the elimination of a destructive trait or the creation of a physical object, you must first plan it out in your mind, then put it on paper. For example, you might write your goals on three-by-five note cards, create a blueprint for a house, and so on. Without these steps, nothing of any value can be created.

"Meditation, then, is the thought process that precedes the accomplishment of any action you pursue, whether it be good or evil. Satan would have you meditate on those things that are destructive to your physical, mental, and spiritual development. Again, you have your agency to choose the path you desire. Choose evil, and your destruction is assured. Choose righteousness, and your salvation is assured."

CHAPTER THIRTEEN

Honesty and Integrity

"Would you please discuss the importance of honesty and integrity?" I asked. "There seems to be a great lack of these traits in today's society."

"Well, now, you hardly let me get a breath before another question comes!" John laughed. "But I know that you believe time is short and we need to get on with answering your questions.

"Honesty is one of the most revered of all personality traits. Employers and people in all walks of life seek those who are honest and forthright in their dealings with others. You can always trust those who are honest. You can depend on them to keep their word and be true to their duties and responsibilities. They do not cheat, lie, or use people in an unrighteous manner. In most instances, they will not betray your trust or your love. Therefore, you can be assured that anything said to them in confidence will stay with them.

"Honesty means being truthful in all your dealings with others, using no deceit, and living your lives so that you have nothing to hide.

"Honesty begins within your minds. In his play *Hamlet*, William Shakespeare advised, 'To thine own self be true.' In other words, being honest with yourself makes it easier to be honest with others.

"Honesty needs to be nurtured from childhood. If it is not learned then, it may be very difficult to incorporate into your life later. The rewards for its development more than compensate for the time and effort expended in its cultivation.

"Honesty is an integral part of repentance. You must always be completely honest with God when you confess your sins, when you seek His forgiveness, or in any of the steps of repentance. Your motives must be honest when you approach baptism or when you ask anything of your Lord and Savior.

"Honesty is not just a black-and-white issue. There is no one who is completely honest, nor is there anyone who is totally dishonest. All humans fall somewhere in between because of their thinking, attitudes, and experiences. That is why you can never completely place your trust in humans. Deity, having infinite honesty, can always be trusted.

"If you are truly on the road to perfection, then you will honestly evaluate yourself to determine where you stand with respect to God-like honesty. You must sincerely make the necessary effort to perfect this most-cherished character trait. You may even ask a family member to evaluate you. Others do not always share the opinion you have of yourself. The way others see you or the way you view yourself may not reflect your true personality. You project yourself the way you want others to see you. You hide from them the things you don't want them to know. You magnify the good and play down the bad.

"On the other hand, you cannot be totally honest with everyone. And you don't need to completely expose your past. It could be detrimental if everyone's pasts were to be revealed. Privacy is important, and some things should be kept confidential. But if you have committed a serious moral indiscretion, you need to confess. Seek out one who is in authority and clear the matter up with God. Part of the reward of true repentance is that God will no longer remember your sins.

"Here is the big question: how do you incorporate this element into your daily life? How do you perfect your honesty? Admitting that you are not scrupulous in everything you do is a good step in the right direction. Then, on a continuing basis, you must analyze the dishonesties you practice daily. As Sir Walter Scott wrote in *Marmion*, 'O what a tangled web we weave, / when first we practice to deceive.'

"Once you become aware of even the little deceitful things you do and say each day, you can start eliminating them from your life.

"Dishonesty stems from an unwillingness to be responsible. When you do something wrong, you often try to hide it from others, and you become afraid. You fear that those whom you love or whom you hold in high esteem will care less for you if they know the truth. You fear that their opinion of you will diminish. So, you lie, deceive, and shy away from being responsible—you become dishonest.

"Honesty takes courage and effort, both to develop and to practice. Satan would have all humans be dishonest. When you understand that dishonesty leads to destruction and comes from the promptings of Satan, you stand a better chance of eliminating it from your life."

John paused for a moment, then continued.

"Now, integrity. This is that quality in you that espouses honesty, moral values, high standards, uprightness, sincerity, and the seeking of perfection in all that you do.

"Like honesty, integrity is one of the most sought-after character traits. People of integrity often are placed in positions of responsibility and leadership because they can be trusted to carry out assigned duties and to be fair in their relationships.

"Integrity should be pursued with intensity and determination in all aspects of life. When you have developed and perfected this trait, you will have progressed on the road to attaining residence with God. He will bless you in many ways in your sincere efforts to master integrity."

CHAPTER FOURTEEN

Loyalty

"Was there anything else that you wanted answered today?" John asked.

"I could keep you here for a month with my questions," I replied. "How about this one: would you please discuss loyalty and to whom we owe our first loyalty?"

"You have really asked some interesting questions today," John laughed. "I can understand why I was sent here.

"Loyalty is the state of being true to your vows, commitments, and obligations, both real and implied. This includes promises made to God, individuals, families, groups, organizations, countries, and global societies. Loyalty should only be demonstrated under righteous circumstances and for righteous purposes. When you are supportive of or condone unrighteous endeavors, you are not being loyal. Rather, you are assuming partial or equal guilt with those who have committed the unrighteous act.

"To be loyal, you must not deny anyone the opportunity for repentance. When the question of loyalty arises, you need to ask yourself, 'Is this productive, nonproductive, or counterproductive to growth toward perfection?' You will not go astray if you are true to

God's commandments and to productivity. It is not difficult to determine where your loyalty should lie when viewed in this light.

"When friends or relatives commit serious crimes, are you serving their best interests when you remain silent? No! You are contributing to their damnation as well as your own. To be loyal to them, you are being disloyal to God and to yourself. Viewed from a righteous standpoint, you can only help when you give others the opportunity for repentance. You cannot do this if you shield them from God's laws or from whatever other justice is being denied. Shielding them denies Christ's atonement and denies them the opportunity to experience His redemptive powers. Your responsibility to those who have committed an infraction should always be to lead them toward repentance. If they refuse, then you must make sure they understand that your obligation lies in doing that which is right in the eyes of God and the law.

"When you fully understand the principle of repentance, you also will know where your loyalty to others ends. When they commit petty transgressions, you must always pray for guidance before acting.

"Loyalty to your country is also important, but not more so than your allegiance to God. You should always be faithful to your country, family, and society, but not at the expense of Christ's redemption. When there arises a choice between God and state, there should be no question of your decision."

John's words recalled another experience from my past.

"I think I understand what you mean," I said. "In 1968, while I was serving in Vietnam, my wife Geri and our children returned to Arizona to stay with Geri's father. One of our sons became infatuated with a young girl in his class. To impress her, he went to the local grocery story and stole as many of the toys hanging on a display that he could stuff into his coat.

"That night Geri discovered his hoard. Knowing that he had no money, she questioned him, only to be told, 'My friend George gave them to me.'

"Geri then asked what George would say if she called him and asked him.

"'He would tell you that he gave them to me,' my son answered.

"'What would his mother say if I asked her?' Geri countered.

"With a bowed head, my son admitted that he had stolen the items, and cried that he was sorry.

"All day Geri prayed about how to handle the situation. After lunch, she went to see the store manager. When she had apprised him of the problem, he asked her what she wanted him to do.

"'I want him to realize that he cannot do this sort of thing,' Geri said. 'I want him to have to pay for these items, and I want him never to do anything like this again!'

"The manager promised to be very cooperative. She didn't realize it then, but the Lord would also turn out to be very cooperative.

"As they pulled into the parking lot that afternoon, two boys came out of the market accompanied by two policemen and the store manager. The boys were marched over to a waiting police car and locked into the back seat. The two officers returned to the store. My son's eyes got as big as saucers.

"'What do you think those boys did?' Geri asked.

"'I don't know,' he said.

"His mother insisted that they go into the grocery store. Our reluctant son followed. The manager and officers were talking about what the store wanted to do about the boys who had been caught shoplifting. The manager said, 'I want them charged so that others will get the message, too.'

"After the officers left, the manager turned to my wife and my son, who was peeking out from behind his mother.

"'Did you want to see me?' he asked Geri. It seemed that his voice was unusually gruff.

"'My son needs to talk to you,' she answered, and pushed the boy forward.

"Not only did our son look scared, but he was also shaking. He opened the sack he was carrying to reveal the stolen items.

"'I took these.' His voice quavered.

"The manager gave the items a cursory glance.

"'Did you see the policemen take those boys out of here?' the manager asked.

"Our son nodded his head.

"'Do you want me to call them back to take you away, too?'

"This time he shook his head no.

"'Well, come into my office and let me think about this,' the manager ordered.

"He added up the price of the items.

"'With tax, they come to $5.43,' he said 'Do you have that much money?'

"My son shook his head no.

"'I have this much,' he said, drawing out some loose change—$1.47.

"'That's not enough,' the manager said. 'Let me tell you what I want you to do. I want you to get a job and earn the money to pay me. I want your money. Not your mother's—yours. After you have paid me, you must never come back into my store alone. I do not let thieves come in here. Do you understand?'

"Up and down went our son's head. Then he reached to pick up the sack, but his mother stopped him.

"'Son, we don't profit from stealing,' Geri said. 'Not only must you give up your money, but you do not get anything to show for its passing.'

"They went home, and that evening our son got a job cutting and weeding a neighbor's lawn. He earned $5.00 and paid his debt that night."

"That's a good example," John said. "When you see someone on the verge of wrongdoing and you remain silent, you are actually denying the offenders the opportunity to repent and work out their salvation. Sometimes it may be difficult for you to help them get back on the right path. But, for the laws of justice and mercy to be effective, you must do what is right, even if it is painful for you and those involved.

"Loyalty also includes supporting others in their righteous endeavors. For you to sit back and watch others struggle to accomplish something with which you also should be in involved, knowing that you should help, is not productive to your growth. Whenever possible, your responsibility is to help others reach their righteous goals. This forms a beautiful bond and helps all involved to work out their salvation.

"The scriptures inform us that Satan's preexistent plan was to force humankind to be righteous, so that not one soul would be lost.

"This plan would have taken away your agency and made you a slave. Christ's plan was to give you the freedom to choose, then teach you the right way and let you choose your path. Everyone who has been born or ever will be born, to one degree or another, chose Christ's plan. In so doing, everyone has the obligation to remain loyal to His plan. Your growth will then be sufficient to allow you to live with God in the Celestial Kingdom. Your loyalty must be to God and to His complete Gospel plan above any other loyalty. This includes all His teachings, laws, commandments, and ordinances. Your loyalty to God commits you to continually strive toward the perfection He has commanded of you (Matt. 5:48), and which is necessary for your salvation and exaltation.

"History is replete with examples of loyalty and misplaced loyalty, including Nathan Hale, who regretted that he had but one life to give to his country; Benedict Arnold, who became a traitor to his country; and the Old Testament prophet Eli, who placed loyalty to his sons above his loyalty to God, resulting in death for Eli and his sons (1 Sam. 4:11-18).

"You have your agency to choose your loyalties. But sometimes, instead of meditating and praying about your priorities, you wait for a crisis before deciding and then you often make the wrong one. When you thoughtfully and prayerfully arrange your priorities in support of righteousness, your decision will automatically be the right one. You won't even have to stop and think about it.

"For most decisions, loyalty to God also encompasses loyalty to your family and loved ones. But sometimes there is a conflict, and doing the right thing is difficult and painful. Nevertheless, if the right decision is made, the Lord will bless all parties concerned."

CHAPTER FIFTEEN

Humility

Now my thoughts turned to other concepts I had often wondered about, such as humility and meekness, and the ideas mentioned in the beatitudes. We are told to be humble, meek, and loyal, but there is no real meaning attached to these words except in the dictionary. But dictionary definitions are not always in complete harmony with the views in the scriptures. If there is no explanation for the true meaning of these and other concepts, how can we really put them into practice? How can we be humble if we don't know the true meaning of humility?

"You have been very helpful in your explanations thus far," I said. "Now, what about terms like 'humility' and 'meekness'? If I go by their dictionary definitions, I'm left with an incomplete picture of what is required to be humble or meek. Could you offer a more realistic and comprehensive explanation of these qualities, so I'll know how to integrate them into my life?"

John paused for a moment before answering. Then he said, "There are many such terms or qualities whose biblical meanings seem to be at odds with their dictionary definitions. I'll discuss these two, but as for the others, you must meditate on them yourself, and the answers will come.

"Humility is the recognition of, and the actions related to, your total dependence on God for anything and everything in this life. With His power and through His Son, Jesus Christ, and the Holy Ghost, He has created and controls all things in the universe. Without their love for you, you would not exist; without your love for them, you would have no reason to exist.

"It is the recognition of, and the actions relating to, the fact that everything in His creation is subject to His will and His desires. Because He is the creator, He is always in complete control of this world. He has a personal interest and love for each of you, regardless of what you have done or who you are. He wants you to perfect your body, mind, and spirit through the atonement and using your agency, whereby you can choose to be obedient to His laws and commandments.

"It is the recognition of, and the actions related to, the fact that God considers all people to be of equal value, regardless of status, position, race, creed, religion, or rank. Any separation that does exist is the result of individual choices, thoughts, and deeds. He blesses all who are obedient to His law. Your joy and happiness depends on your manifesting love for others. Lack of humility is obvious in human pride and in the many atrocities' humans commit against one another.

"It is the recognition that everyone has faults and imperfections. Your deficiencies are given to refine you and make you aware that you are unable to become perfect and attain salvation without the aid of your Father in heaven and of Jesus Christ. You must accept the fact that no one is perfect. Therefore, you must be tolerant of the imperfections you see in others and encourage them toward perfection in an atmosphere of love and kindness.

"Humbling yourself before God means not only recognizing Him, but also loving, obeying, and serving Him, and knowing that every blessing flows from Him. To be humble can be very difficult because you must treat everyone equally. It is not right to place yourself above or below others, regardless of your status. You are no better than anyone else, and no one else is better than you no matter what you both do or what you have. Therefore, you can learn from everyone, and you have something to teach everyone.

"Humility is the recognition that God exists, that He is the architect of the creation of this world, and that you, as part of this creation, are subject to His laws and rules. Obedience or disobedience to these laws and rules subjects you to blessings and punishments. Participation in His ordinances are symbolic of your acceptance of and love for Him.

"It is the recognition that Jesus Christ, under the direction of His Father, is the creator of this world and that He is the only mediator between humankind and God. Upon your repentance, Jesus is the Redeemer, the only one who can cleanse you of your sins and bring you back into the presence of God.

"As for meekness," John concluded, "this means to be gentle, kind, loving, mild of temper, and submissive to God's commandments. But contrary to popular belief, meekness is not weakness. Rather, it is courage to face the world from a position of strength and resolve, embracing love and rejecting evil."

CHAPTER SIXTEEN

Forgiveness and Unforgiveness

We stopped to rest on an outcropping of rock as we paused at the pass overlooking Ptarmigan Lake. Some ducks were swimming around, occasionally diving for food. It was quiet and serene, one of the most peaceful scenes I had observed in the Rockies,

I somehow sensed that our communication was nearing an end. With all this input, my overtaxed brain was beginning to feel fuzzy around the edges. I found it very difficult to concentrate on my next question.

After gathering my thoughts, I finally asked, "Next to love and charity, what is the most important quality to develop or embrace in this life?"

Without any hesitation, John answered, "Forgiveness! Everyone will offend someone at one time or another in this life, sometimes deliberately: sometimes unintentionally. When you refuse to forgive someone for a trespass, it produces more pain, anguish, and soul destruction for you than for whoever committed the offense. It is one more burden that *you have elected* to carry, one more event added to an ever-increasing load of unneeded personal baggage. This leads to illness, misery, and unhappiness. It also denies Christ's atonement. In effect, you are saying that you would rather do the atonement yourself—which, of course, you can't.

"Since forgiveness is an element of love and unity, then unforgiveness is an element of hate and disunity. Unforgiveness is a spiritual stress that affects both the mind and the body, and that interferes with normal healing and life processes. Forgiveness is releasing and cleansing oneself of either trying to avoid responsibility or to assume the blame for another's actions. No matter how hard you try, you cannot be liable for what others do. When you believe others have done wrong, and you make a judgment or form a belief, then you are trying to assume responsibility for the creation of their lives. However, you *can* make a judgment that you will not do what they have done.

"You can't live another's life according to the concepts you have formed in your mind. When you conclude or form a belief that someone else should act or do things *your way,* you have created an unforgiveness that needs to be resolved. Your inability to control other people's lives or the way they act creates stress within you. This stress is in direct opposition to the life force that resides within your form, your temple of God. The more unforgiveness you harbor, the greater the opposition to this life force, and the more apt you are to become ill and spiritually unresponsive. The same holds true when you embrace or express any of the elements of disunity, disharmony, and hate."

He paused for a moment before continuing.

"God teaches that if you can't or won't forgive, then you cannot be forgiven (Luke 6:37). How could you possibly expect to reside with God when you cling to any unforgiveness? It pollutes your soul and is in opposition to love and unity. Since God is love and you are attempting to become like Him, then you must rid yourself of any element that is in opposition to love. The life force of God is love and harmony, and the opposing forces of hate and disunity cannot coexist with Him. That is why you must be completely cleansed of all your imperfections and be sanctified, through repentance, and baptism, before you can reside with God. Turn all your unforgiveness over to Christ. He died for the opportunity to assume your sins. Try as you might, you cannot assume this responsibility for yourself—or for anyone else. Forgiveness is an element of repentance, which you would do well to study in depth.

"Self-forgiveness is no different. How can you expect God to forgive you when you won't forgive yourself? If you ask Him for forgiveness but then insist on holding on to all your guilt and judgments, you can't expect to be cleansed. Forgiveness is the releasing and washing away of the responsibility for a thought or action that is detrimental to your growth toward the Celestial Kingdom of God. Christ can help you with the release, but He cannot do it for you. Only when you have turned it over to Him can you be forgiven.

"The most troubling problems in the world are the result of unforgiveness between individuals, organizations, and nations. Forgiveness is a cleansing, and purifying, based in love, a releasing of the responsibility for a thought or action. When this is accomplished and repentance is true, you can rise above the necessity to repeat the thought or action.

"This world is on the verge of many great cataclysms and upheavals that will literally change the face of the earth and the heavens. Those who are found to have unforgiveness in their hearts will not be caught up with Christ to reign with Him. Only those who are pure in heart, mind, and soul—the sanctified, the repentant, the innocent— will be allowed in His kingdom. This world has very little time in which to prepare for Christ's second coming. There are very few who will heed these warnings and embrace the concepts necessary to bring them back into the grace of God. Getting past the attachments, the collectibles, and the need to have fun or be entertained every minute in this life is impossible for most. Of those who eventually come to read this, only a small fraction will be motivated to take any action. It is for those few that these words have been given."

CHAPTER SEVENTEEN

Know Your Enemy

"I feel that our time together is about to end," I said, a little desperately, "so please, will you discuss our enemy Satan so that others may know that He is the only true enemy we have on the face of this earth?"

"I really don't mind answering one last question," John smiled. "After all, that's why I came here today."

"When God created this world, He chose to allow Satan and his followers to tempt His children, but not to take full control of their lives. If God were to allow this to happen, His children would be totally at the mercy of Satan and would have no opportunity to return to God and also chose to give His children the Holy Spirit and guardian angels to offset the temptations of Satan. To understand this more fully, I need to tell you how Satan influences you.

"The still, small voice you hear that tells you when you are doing wrong? That is the mental communication from either God's angels or the Holy Spirit. The one who is influencing you to do wrong is Satan. He uses his persuasive mental powers to tell you that something wrong, is all right and will benefit you or give you happiness. Deception is what he does, clouding your minds to the truth. He also influences your emotions and your use of the elements of love and hate, magnifying hate or diminishing love so there effects on you will suit his purposes.

"Lucifer was cast out with a third of the hosts of heaven, and He and his fallen angels became your mortal enemies. He then swore to destroy you by using every means at his disposal. It matters not if you are righteous or if you completely embrace His evil ways. Even if you were to worship him as a god, he has still sworn your destruction because we humans did not follow him in his rebellion against God.

"You are his enemy, and he is continually striving to destroy you and make you as miserable as he is. You must recognize that he is at war with you. If you are to survive and attain the highest degree of glory in God's kingdom, you must fight back by declaring and waging a winning war against him and his evil legions here on earth. You must study your enemy to grasp how he uses people to do his bidding. You must learn to see through his lies and understand exactly how he plans your destruction. You must understand that it is Satan who creates contention, strife, bigotry, prejudice, hatred, greed, and anger in human hearts—elements which make all of you slaves to his evil designs.

"You must never become complacent about Satan's power. He uses his power every second of every day to gradually bring you, both directly and indirectly, under his control. To minimize his efforts, you must develop a righteous plan of action based on the scriptures and the revealed words of the prophets. God does not intend for you to fight this battle alone. In humility, you must learn to rely on His help and His priesthood to win.

"To understand the magnitude of Satan's efforts, you must examine the great and small evils that have befallen humanity down through the ages. They are all Satan's doing. Look at all the evils that exist in the world today. Who perpetrated the evils that led to the necessity of the flood in Noah's time? Look at Sodom and Gomorrah, and at the mass destruction of the Jews by Hitler. Take a good look at the terrorists that you allow to exist in the world today. Do you enjoy these great evils?

"Why are you humans so vulnerable to Satan? It's not because you love misery. It's just that you have not yet learned how to recognize and turn away from Satan's promptings. Perhaps you haven't bothered to learn how he operates or attacks. You may not even know your own areas of vulnerability. Many of you won't even acknowledge that you respond to him to any significant degree, or even allow that you are at war with him. Maybe it is too painful for you to admit that you often fight on his side. To do so would be too much for you to handle, so you just ignore him and try to justify your actions with lame excuses. So, you humans become his puppets, his dupes, his soldiers, doing his bidding, all because you just can't be bothered to take the steps God has outlined in the scriptures to protect you against the powers of evil. You have not yet learned to hear the whisperings of the Holy Spirit and take the appropriate action. Yet you react when Satan influences someone to hurt you. You often allow your emotions to be magnified out of proportion. You give way to greed, anger, hatred, lust, and other destructive traits for your own selfish desires, which Satan has created. You cast aside the righteous teachings of your parents, your ecclesiastical leaders, and society for the pleasures of the world. You become fun-seeking, gratification-minded procrastinators.

"Many of you are passive to the evils that exist in the world. Your complacency is necessary so that you won't have to do anything about this world in which you live. Why are you humans like this? Is it because Satan makes it acceptable, attractive, and enjoyable? This enjoyment is only a facade that hides the misery of disobedience," John declared.

I was quite taken aback by the way he made everything so personal, as if he were talking directly to me. But I had to admit that what he said was true, and that perhaps we should all take it personally.

"Surely Satan doesn't have that much power over the people of the world?" I countered. "Yet, when I look back on the major wars of my lifetime, I must admit that I am amazed at the gullibility of the people of all nations. We all stand ready and willing to believe anything and everything the media and our governments feed us. The lies, deceits, and propaganda we so readily accept and react to cannot come from God. The media and the governments, under Satan's influence, makes it so easy and acceptable to kill and torture other human beings, all for the power and greed of those who embrace evil and seek, power, dominance, and wealth. This is Satan's work, to use people as weapons to destroy each other. Why do we let the media and the governments do this? We never seem to learn. History has given us this lesson for thousands of years, and we still haven't learned. War was never created to protect us from another nation, although at times we must protect ourselves. War was created by the greedy to gain power over others at the promptings of Satan. Those who use war to get power or satisfy their greedy natures realize that we must protect ourselves from others, and so they exploit this knowledge for their own purposes. We, as citizens of all nations, become dupes in these great perpetrations of evil. We are pawns, and we reap the pain, death, and destruction that should fall on those powers behind the governments that are responsible for the wars. In essence, though, it is Satan who breeds the greed and selfishness in those who use us."

"Those powers behind the governments do not realize that they are losing far more than are you who are their puppets," John warned. "They are responsible for their own salvation, growth, and progress here on earth, and when they choose to respond to the promptings of Satan to such a degree, they are lost. The reward for their great evil is nothing but wealth and power while they are on earth. At death, their wealth and power are lost to them, along with the opportunity to reside with God throughout the eternities. The reward for their evil is eternal misery with no hope. One of the greatest evils is that these power-hungry puppets of Satan pass their wealth and power to their heirs, who carry forth the legacy of their parents. Is the power and wealth gained in this short lifetime worth eternal punishment? I think not!

"So, you must learn Satan's strategies, weaknesses, and strengths. Learn how He strikes and what weapons are most effective against him. You must realize that Satan is your only true enemy on this earth and direct your energies accordingly.

"You should then create an alarm system within you that will warn you when you react adversely to life's many trying situations. This will help you win the war. Your energies should be channeled into increasing your love for others, regardless of who they are. Love is the greatest weapon God has given you with which to fight Satan. It is God's ultimate law, and those of you who embrace it create little islands of peace in the world that help to negate the evils around you.

"Satan's attempt to destroy you never ceases. Your efforts to prevent this destruction also should never cease. You need to be on guard against his onslaught every wakeful moment. When hurts and anger swell within you, realize from whence they come. Until you realize this, you will vent your frustrations on those who are acting as Satan's servants at the moment. It is easy to respond to anger with anger or to hatred with hatred. When God commanded you to love your enemies, He was telling you to respond to all situations created by Satan with love and kindness, not retaliation. Whose side are you on when you respond to anger with anger or hatred with hatred? Certainly not God's!

"You may believe that Satan only prompts you to do evil things, but you also must realize that he magnifies your destructive emotions such as lust, greed, envy, and all other nonproductive and counter-productive elements and characteristics. He is relentless in his pursuit to destroy you. When you get miffed at someone, he will magnify this into anger, and anger into hatred—if you let him. He also will exert every effort to dampen and diminish the love, compassion, humility, and all other productive elements so that they will have less of an effect on their recipients. Don't ever be fooled into believing that Satan has little power to influence your actions. That is exactly what he wants you to believe.

"When you win a battle against anger or prejudice, Satan would have you believe that *you* have won the war. He will lull you into a sense of false security by easing up on that area, then quietly go to another weakness that you have left unguarded. Then, if you allow it, he will slowly drag you down to destruction. Many times, you won't even realize you are being attacked until it is too late, or almost too late. Satan's greatest weapons are his patience and persistence. He will never give up, regardless of who you are. His efforts start when you are born and do not cease until you die. He works on your parents, your friends, your peers, and your enemies to bombard you with his unholy influences. He subtly tries to make every vice, every destructive element, and every evil acceptable. Absolutely nothing is sacred to him. He is at war with you, and everything goes.

"So, what can you do to counter this everlastingly evil onslaught? You certainly cannot counter it alone! You must rely on the only source available: God's plan of salvation, the Gospel of Jesus Christ.

"The magnitude of the laws of love cannot be overplayed. The basic premise is that humans are never enemies of one another, regardless of the situation. I know this is hard to accept when someone threatens your life, or the lives of your loved ones, but you must look past the threat and realize that Satan is behind the scenes and has created the situation. '"Vengeance is mine; I will repay," saith the Lord' (Rom. 12:19). To purify yourselves, you must react only in love and understanding to any situation that comes into your lives. That is the ultimate aim of those who would be perfect. Relying on the Holy Spirit and having faith in Jesus Christ can see you through any situation. This doesn't mean that you shouldn't protect yourself or your loved ones from attack. Just realize that it started with Satan.

"One of the big problems humans have is the tendency to fight fire with fire, anger with anger, prejudice with prejudice, or hatred with hatred. But 'an eye for an eye' was supplanted by Christ's teachings. How much better and less traumatic to fight anger with love, hatred with love, prejudice with love, and so on.

"God never said it would be *easy* to follow His path in this chaotic world, just *necessary* if you wish to gain residence with Him in the Celestial Kingdom. Just remember that the only thing standing between your love and friendship for one another is the enmity placed there by Satan. He gives you millions of excuses not to love one another—just excuses, not reasons. There are no valid reasons for *not* loving one another, but thousands of good reasons *for* loving one another. By overcoming them, all our trials and tribulations refine us and bring us closer to God.

"If you, as the human race, could only recognize that Satan and his legions are responsible for of all the pain, misery, and destruction in the world, and if you would use the weapons God has given you to counter the evil one, then you could almost completely eliminate the misery in the world. Satan is fully armed and committed to your destruction—physical, mental, emotional, and spiritual. He will spare no effort; he will use any tool, weapon, or person in his control—with your permission—to bring about your destruction. His helpers are the third of the hosts of heaven—the fallen angels, who are as dedicated as he is to your spiritual demise. If he has his way, not one of you will be spared. His greatest targets are love, your agency and all righteous characteristics, traits, and attributes. You must never let your guard down and allow him the pleasure of your destruction.

"Another of Satan's major goals is to destroy your physical bodies. He does this in many ways. For example, he influences those in your food industry to put additives, dyes, flavor enhancers, destructive chemicals, and the like into your foods, which ultimately lead to illness. There have been so many drugs, remedies, and additives included in what you take into your bodies that it would be impossible to name them all. God wants you to use your intelligence to learn all you can about foods, herbs, vitamins, and supplements so that you can, with wisdom, control your own health and well-being.

"But Satan prompts you to ignore the laws of nutrition. He does not want you to know which foods keep you healthy. He wants you to put your faith in humans as far as nutrition is concerned. After all, people are not interested in making money; they're just interested in helping you to be healthy, right? How can you expect to remain healthy if you do not study the laws of nutrition? For every obedience to the law, there is a blessing! Obedience to the laws of health can prevent many of the illnesses in todays world. Information is available to prevent most of these illnesses if you will but search for it. It is easy to be misled by some of the books available, but you have our Lord on your side to help you. You also have the wisdom God gave you. If the laws of health are studied and closely followed, you will not only remain healthy, but you can overcome many of the diseases you have accumulated by disobedience to the laws of health. If you really want to see the influence of Satan, look at the drug and alcohol problems around the world. And you *allow* Satan to do this to you? The bottom line is that you should be at war with Satan, not each other.

"God has not left you to fight the war alone. The scriptures show you what weapons are most effective in defeating Satan. They were ordained for your use. You have no weapons other than those God has given you. Allow God to be your general in this terrible war Satan is waging against you. There is no other way to win. Your salvation depends on it."

John was silent for a while, either waiting for me to say something or perhaps to collect his thoughts. I was too stunned to say a word. The impact on my emotions was so great that I had to take a moment and allow what he had said to sink in. But before I could say anything, he spoke again. He repeated some of what he had stated before, as if to emphasize the points.

"Most of you," he continued, "are aware that Satan uses people to bring pain and misery into the world, but you are reluctant to admit that he uses you for these same purposes, and that you often willingly become his slaves, doing his bidding even against your better judgment. When you yield to his temptations, you retard your growth and the growth of those against whom you sin, perhaps affecting their acceptance of the Gospel and Jesus Christ as their Savior. Thus, your actions may have an eternal effect on the lives of others. The guilt and repercussions created by giving in to Satan's temptations will affect your spirituality for eternity—unless you take advantage of your Savior's atonement, and repent. Each sin you commit has many tentacles that not only affect your lives, but also the lives of those around you. This is all part of Satan's plan in his war against you.

"This war against humankind has been going on for about 6,000 years. It began even before Eve partook of the forbidden fruit in the Garden of Eden. It began in the spirit world when Satan and his followers failed in their attempt to entice humans to rebel against God. Satan has since honed his skills as a battle-hardened force of destruction, targeting *everyone* born into this world. The only person strong enough to resist all his temptations was our Savior, Jesus Christ. Everyone else has, at times, been seduced by Satan's urges, his promptings, his lies, and his promises of pleasure and wealth in his rampage of destruction.

"When Satan can induce anyone to do his bidding, he has won a battle. Why are you humans so ready to respond? Why are you enticed to believe that evil, in any form, is pleasurable or even acceptable to God, and that Satan's ways can bring happiness to you? Why do you often revel in bringing misery to others? The answers to these questions are not simple.

"Few of you would murder at the first provocation, but Satan can gradually take you down the long road of evil by enticing you to give in to his temptations, one at a time, until finally you are ready to kill. It may be your temper, anger, greed, or some other trait that he works on until finally you are completely under his control. Satan would have you believe that this loss of control is acceptable—and even desirable, in some societies.

"There are those in the world who do not believe in a God or a supreme being. I would ask them one question. What evidence exists that there is no Supreme Being when everything in God's creation points to an intelligent creator? God is the creator of all things. Most scientists now agree that this world and this universe could not have just happened. There had to be an intelligent intervention. And just because you don't believe in God does not mean that you will be exempt from the judgment. Think very deeply about this and change your thinking, or you will be held accountable to God's justice and will have no part in Christ's mercy.

"To be a winner in this war against Satan, you must constantly be on guard. Study and learn the methods and weapons he uses to bring about your destruction. Then you must learn to use the weapons God has given you to counter every move Satan makes. You must always be alert to new thrusts and temptations so that you can protect yourself from him. The impact of Satan's influence must never be underestimated, or he will win most of his battles. He is committed to your physical, mental, emotional, and spiritual destruction. He doesn't worry about making a living, taking vacations, sleeping, taking care of a family, or anything but devoting all his time, energy, and resources to your downfall—if you allow it.

"Your only hope in winning this war is to listen to the counsel of God in the scriptures and among your prophets. You also must fast and pray for God's help, then meditate and listen to His answer. You must accept and follow the law of repentance because it neutralizes the sins Satan has enticed you to commit. The law of repentance is so important that Satan will devote much of his time to convincing you that it is worthless, that your sins are too great to be forgiven, that there is no such thing as sin, that it won't do any good anyway ... Christ was only a teacher, not your redeemer ... that Christ doesn't even exist.

"Satan plants these and other lies in your hearts and minds to confuse you and lead you astray. He would have you believe that other channels are available for your salvation besides those provided by the Gospel. When you respond to Satan's influence and disobey God's commandments, it is imperative that you repent, or you cannot be forgiven. Satan would have you believe that you are lost when you have committed some grievous sin, that there is no longer a need to strive toward perfection. This is not so. Your Savior died for your sins, but they are only wiped clean when you repent and persevere in your efforts to progress and become perfect.

"To prevent you from repenting, Satan will create fear within you. This may be fear of punishment or of retribution, fear that others will look down on you, fear of being rejected, and so on. He will use all your fears and everything else at his disposal to keep you from repenting.

"The only way to overcome your fears is by developing courage. You must pray for it and seek counsel from your friends and family for sustaining strength and support, and from your church leaders, to whom you must go anyway to confess. What do you have to gain by being courageous? Eternal life, forgiveness, joy, and happiness! What do you lose if you fail to develop and use your courage? You reap everlasting misery, pain, sorrow, and illness. Christ will not forgive you if you do not seek repentance and baptism. So, which is the best choice? Through fasting and prayer, courage will most certainly come. These steps cannot be circumvented; they are necessary for your salvation and exaltation."

John paused again and contemplated what he would say next.

I was completely overcome and wished he would say no more—but more was to come.

He continued, "How much power does Satan have over your life? Just as much as God and you allow! Satan cannot take your life directly. However, He can certainly shorten it indirectly by influencing you to pollute your mind and body with drugs, alcohol, overeating, cigarettes, and so on. He also can influence you to commit murder and mayhem by causing you to lose control of your temper or your wits, or by allowing greed and the other elements of hate to control your lives.

"Whether you admit it or not, there *is* a war going on between good and evil. Choosing the side on which you will fight is not just a one-time choice. It is a choice you must make every minute of every day. It is a choice you make for the continuation of every thought that comes into your heads. If the thought is counterproductive to your growth and you continue to pursue it, then you have chosen Satan's side of the war for that specific moment. The more often you choose the wrong thoughts to pursue, the easier it becomes to give in to these thoughts the next time. Slowly you are drawn into a web of sin to which you soon become a slave. You become one of Satan's soldiers, to be used at his discretion, not yours.

"*You are at war*, a war that most people won't admit to or recognize. It is a one-sided war because most people don't take the time or make the effort to understand what this life is all about. They don't want to hear about it, or they don't have time to be bothered. Even members of the many churches around the world are not as knowledgeable as they should be about this war. They don't develop the weapons they need to fight a winning battle. They don't even bother to find out which weapons are available or effective. They get so caught up in their own little worlds that they refuse to see what's going on.

"Lucifer, Son of the Morning, the fallen angel, the ruler of the kingdom of hell, has taken the time to know what your weaknesses are, and how to battle each one of you. Are you then to fight him alone, without generating the greatest opposition of which you are capable? Will he let you alone if you don't fight back? Not on your eternal life he won't! He is dead serious about what he is trying to do to you. Be just as serious and carry the fight to his side for a change.

Don't fight alone but muster the greatest army this world has ever known: an army of saints, who, with the power of God on their side, can and will win!

"This war cannot be won by standing on the sidelines or sitting on the fence. Those who do this have joined the ranks of Satan. To win, you must use the weapons of faith, hope, justice, mercy, humility, love, charity, righteousness, service, meekness, repentance, and all other productive traits. Include the priesthood of God, and this war can be won by all of you. God will bless your efforts to this end without fail.

"You must create an image in your minds of Satan gnashing his teeth and throwing temper tantrums when you resist one of his temptations or do a charitable deed for someone. Every time you reach a productive goal, visualize his discomfort and the joy of your Father in heaven. Doing this will help to reinforce your commitment to the war against the evil one.

"It is not enough to just lightly study the tools and weapons Satan uses against you. *You must study with all your hearts and meditate on these things.* Individually and collectively, you are involved in this war. No one is excluded, and although many of you have already joined the ranks of Satan, it is never too late to switch to the side of those who will ultimately win. To join God's ranks, you must repent, and you must endure to the end.

"This war is real and deadly. Just because you hear no bombs exploding or shots being fired does not mean it should be taken lightly, or you will lose. There have been far too many casualties already. Let not the next casualty be you."

With that, John departed, leaving me completely speechless and wondering what I should do next.

Appendix

[1]*Author's note: Below is a more complete list of the elements of love and hate. It is my prayer that everyone who reads this work will take it seriously and do what needs to be done for their salvation.* May God bless you all.

Abundance, achievement, activity, agreeableness, ambition, appreciation, affection, assurance, awareness, beauty, benevolence, boldness, bravery, caring, challenge, change, charity, chastity, cleanliness, commitment, compassion, confidence, consideration, consistency, courage, creativity, dedication, detachment, dignity, diligence, discernment, durability, empathy, encouragement, equality, expectation, faith, focus, forgiveness, freedom, friendliness, gentleness, genuineness, giving, goal-centeredness, gratitude, healing, helpfulness, honesty, honor, hope, humility, industry, insight, innocence, integrity, inquisitiveness, interest, intelligence, justice, kindness, knowledge, love, loyalty, mercy, meditation, meekness, modesty, morality, motivation, nonviolence, obedience, organization, open-mindedness, patience, perseverance, persistence, prayerfulness, preparedness, promptness, purity, release, remorse, repentance, resolution, respect, responsibility, reverence, righteousness, sacrifice, self-discipline, self-reliance, sensitivity, spirituality, stability, steadfastness, strength, studiousness, success-centeredness, searching, self-control, self-esteem, surrender, sympathy, tact, temperance, tenderness, thankfulness, thoughtfulness, thrift, tolerance, trustworthiness, truthfulness, understanding, virtue, watchfulness, wisdom, warmth.

This is a more complete list of the elements of hatred, disunity, destruction, disorder, and chaos:

Aggression, anger, apathy, arrogance, attachment, avarice, blindness, blame, callousness, cheating, coldness, contempt, contention, cowardice, crassness, cruelty, deceit, deception, devilishness, discouragement, disagreeableness, disinterest, dishonesty, disloyalty, disobedience, disorderliness, disorganization, disrespect, disdain, destructiveness, doubt, egotism, enmity, envy, evil, faithlessness, fighting, filthiness, foolishness, fun-seeking, giving up, gossiping, greed, hardheartedness, haughtiness, hindrance, hostility, idleness, ignobility, ignorance, immodesty, immorality, impatience, inaction, inadequacy, inconsistency, inconsiderateness, indifference, indolence, indulgence, inequality, ingratitude, injustice, insecurity, intemperateness, intolerance, irreverence, irresponsibility, insensitivity, insincerity, jealousy, judgment, laziness, lust, lying, malevolence, malice, materialism, meanness, mercilessness, negativity, nondependence, nonempathy, nonpersistence, nonseeking, passivity, pollution, prejudice, pride, procrastination, rebelliousness, retaliation, revengefulness, roughness, self-gratification, scarcity-orientation, self-centeredness, selfishness, self-love, self-pity, sloppiness, sloth, tactlessness, thoughtlessness, timidity, ugliness, uncaring, unchastity, uncommittedness, uncreativity, undedication, undiscernment, undiscipline, unforgiveness, unlawfulness, unmeditativeness unmotivation, unprayerfulness, unpreparedness, unrepentance, unrighteousness, unskillfullness, unsuccessfulness, unsurity, unteachableness, untrustworthiness, unvirtuousness, vacillation, vengefulness, violence, weakness.